D0875651

The Cowpuncher

**Center Point
Large Print**

Also by Bradford Scott and available from Center Point Large Print:

Panhandle Pioneer

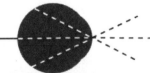

This Large Print Book carries the Seal of Approval of N.A.V.H.

The Cowpuncher

BRADFORD SCOTT

CENTER POINT LARGE PRINT
THORNDIKE, MAINE

This Center Point Large Print edition
is published in the year 2010 by arrangement with
Golden West Literary Agency

The text of this Large Print edition is unabridged.
In other aspects, this book may vary
from the original edition.
Printed in the United States of America.
Set in 16-point Times New Roman type.

ISBN: 978-1-60285-737-7

Library of Congress Cataloging-in-Publication Data

Scott, Bradford, 1893–1975.
  The cowpuncher / Bradford Scott. — Center Point large print ed.
      p. cm.
  ISBN 978-1-60285-737-7 (lib. bnd. : alk. paper)
  1. Cowboys—Fiction. 2. Miners—Fiction. 3. Mines and mineral resources—Fiction.
   4. Frontier and pioneer life—Texas—Fiction. 5. Large type books. I. Title.
  PS3537.C9265C69 2010
    813′.52—dc22
  2009048074

The Cowpuncher

Prologue

Black and ominous against the white fire of the full moon, a crag fanged into the silver blue of the Colorado sky. Far below, a black gorge glowered between its crowding walls of stone. Silent, apparently deserted, lip full of shadows, its rimrock frosted by pale light, it lay like a sullen pool of dark water, yawning like a newly dug grave.

And it was a grave—a place of death and agony, of greed and hate and vengeance to come. A grave, with the towering crag rearing like a gaunt tombstone and the watcher upon the crag like a devilish spirit of evil brooding over the deeds done under the blanket of darkness.

Sinister-beautiful was the watcher, with eyes of fire and a coat of tawny velvet. Fangs as white as the moonlight glistened as a lip lifted in a soundless snarl. The tip of the long tail twitched incessantly. Great muscles, long and lithe, bunched beneath the glossy coat. Razor-edged claws scraped the stone.

The panther was unflaggingly interested in something going on in the gorge. Ears, attuned to catch the *cheep* of the field mouse in its burrow or the mounting of the sap in the tree-trunk, pricked stiffly forward as inexplicable sounds drifted up from the darkness. Knife-keen eyes glowed with a fiercer fire as a faint waver of light appeared on the far-off canyon floor below. The panther's lips drooled as the smell of meat arose to his sensitive nostrils. His paws worked up and down; his hind quarters tensed.

Then, a flickering shadow in the moonlight, he went backward off the crag, landed on his madly clawing pads and tore furiously down the mountainside. He was hundreds of feet away from his previous dizzy perch before the crashing echoes of the explosion left off, leaping from crag to crag. The panther knew instinctively that death was there in that dark valley—horrible lingering death—and he fled from it madly, his nerves twanging at the burst of mansound.

Following the explosion came a moment of tingling silence—a silence broken by a rushing murmur that swiftly grew to a steady roar. The panther snarled over his shoulder at the unaccustomed sound and fled the faster.

Where the mouth of the gorge opened out upon the mesa, a clanking column paused at the sound of the distant explosion. Leading the column was a tall man who wore a helmet of glittering steel. He was slim, straight as a lance, bearded and swarthy. Pride sat upon his high-nosed face, pride and cruelty and ruthlessness. His eyes, black and glittering, burned with a fanatic light. His sinewy hand rested upon the hilt of his sword in its jeweled scabbard.

Beside him walked a man equally tall, equally spare, garbed from head to foot in somber black. Hemp sandals shod his soles, a small black cap sat on his tonsured head. The hair that curled from beneath the cap was white as new-fallen snow. His features were deeply lined and tormented; his eyes burned with innate kindness and an unutterable melancholy. He trembled visibly as the boom of the explosion throbbed upon the sultry air. Turning his fretted gaze upon the tall Spaniard, he spoke in a voice quivering with emotion:

"A fitting climax indeed, Don Fernando, of blood and cruelty and persecution and murder. For this deed, generations yet unborn will curse your name. Why could you not show at least one final gesture of mercy toward these humble people you have so greatly wronged?"

"Peace!" commanded the soldier in a harshly resonant voice. "Tell your beads, Father, and con your psalter, but do not come between me and those whom the king has given me!"

"God help them!" cried the old priest. "A higher king than yours has given them *me,* and I tell you, Don Fernando de Castro, that you have sinned greatly in your dealing with these poor savages and that the hour will come—nay, may even now be at hand—when God's finger will be heavy upon you for the evil you have so lightly done!"

He turned and plodded wearily down the dim trail. With a muttered curse the hidalgo glared after him, and callous as he was, he shivered at the ring in the priest's ominous words—a premonitory trembling, perhaps, brought on by the icy breath of a dark wing brushing the face of the doomed.

Behind the hidalgo clanked the column of armed men, glancing nervously at the dark and wooded slopes on either hand. To one side rushed a swift stream. On the other pushed dense thickets of chaparral. Overhead a dark cloud drifted across the face of the moon and the warm night seemed to turn chill with a strange, unnatural cold. An owl hooted with a weird, screaming note. A frog croaked hoarsely.

Following the armed column was a long mule train bearing heavy burdens that gave out a dull, metallic clanging. From time to time the patient pack-animals lifted attentive ears to some tiny sound that escaped the duller perceptions of the drivers. Now and then they cast apprehensive glances toward the dark slopes ahead. They gave startled squeals as lurid jets of fire spurted unexpectedly from the darkness.

The column was taken by complete surprise. Yells of terror answered the sullen boom of the old smooth-bores and the sharp whistle of unseen arrows. From the thickets on either side rose a weird, whickering screech, pulsing and ululating, racking the brain and numbing the heart. It seemed to coil around and stifle the commands roared by the tall leader.

Ringed by flickering fire and whistling death, the Spaniards fought bravely against the hidden foe, and bravely died. Dark figures leaped from the shadows, ponderous axes rose and fell, ringing loudly on the mail, smashing through the metal, cleaving poorly protected joints, gouging out a crimson flood wherever the white flesh glimmered in the veiled and clamorous moonlight.

The tall hidalgo, his sword a flickering flame, died like a cornered wolf fanging his teeth at death, a ring of his dead around him, slaying a final foe with a convulsive impulse of the muscles even after death had claimed him. The wounded died groaning under the thud of vicious axes reddened to the hand-grips.

With harsh gutturals, the grim *Indios* of the mountains, their vengeance complete, drove off the loaded mules. Silence again fell upon the dark slopes, the lonely silence of the dead.

But not all life was stilled on that bloody battlefield. Deep in a dense thicket a little way up the slope a still-breathing figure lay; and crouched beside it, animal eyes striving to pierce the gloom, atavistic ears interpreting truly the faintest sound, a second figure pulsed with lusty though sluggish life.

The old priest was horribly wounded. Blood dabbled his snowy hair. Blood stained the breast of his robe. He was unconscious, breathing stertoriously. The dull-witted Mexican boy, his personal attendant who followed him with dog-like devotion, was unhurt. With desperate strength and animal cunning, he had snatched his master from the field, eluded the sharpened perceptions of foes far keener than he, and brought him to precarious safety.

Silently the Mexican boy slipped away, and brought back water to quench the padre's thirst and bathe his burning brow. For long minutes the priest lay silent and motionless, thoughts speeding through his brain, the mind tasting the clearness of approaching death. And with those thoughts crystallized what he conceived to be his last duty to the men of his blood and to his king beyond the seas. He signaled the boy to raise him in his arms.

Fumbling with trembling fingers, he ripped a large piece of cloth from his linen under-tunic. He muttered a word and the Mexican boy reached out and broke a long mesquite thorn.

The priest took the thorn, glanced about uncertainly, then scratched his arm deeply with the point. Blood welled from the wound. The priest dipped the thorn into the red stream and pain-fully began to trace lines upon the linen.

For a long time he worked, pausing often to rest as his hand grew feebler and his eye dim. Finally he was finished. He folded the linen with shaking fingers and passed it to the boy.

"To the Officer of the King. Only to the Officer of the King," he commanded.

"To the Officer of the King," parroted the youth. "To the Officer of the King."

With a sigh Padre Diego Escalante sank back, his duty done, and closed his weary eyes. He knew that the boy would neither forget, nor dis-obey. Only to the Spanish governor would he relinquish what Padre Diego had written in blood, telling its story of blood and treasure.

Dusk was falling when the Mexican boy glanced for the last time at the silent figure with the thin hands peacefully folded upon the cavernous breast. Then, like the animals to which he was so nearly kin, he slipped from the thicket to begin his long journey toward where the Officer of the King had his dwelling beside the shallow waters of the Rio Grande.

He did not know, as his masters had not known, that the wrath of an outraged and exploited people had swept the King's officers from the land, nor did any remain to whom he could deliver the message penned by a dying hand.

And back in the somber gorge was silence broken only by the wailing of the lonely wind and the rush and thunder of waters. The brooding walls of the canyon guarded well their dread secret. A secret known now by none who lived in the peaceful moonlight and breathed the sweet night air.

I

Long Way to Texas

Huck Brannon had a headache. A regular skookum he-wolf of a headache—the kind that hopped about inside the head, leaping from brain cell to brain cell on hobnailed boots, crashing against the ceiling of his skull with spiked mallets and kicking an occasional iron hoof at sensitive nerve-centers for good measure. It was a headache worthy of the labor he had done to acquire it.

And the headache was just about all he could call his own in the whole world. An inventory of his pockets revealed them as empty as the belly of a yearlin' after a hard blizzard. His store clothes, which he had put on for his stopover in K.C., after delivery of the herd, were crumpled, stained, dusty, and showed abundant indications of hard wear and sleeping in unconventional places.

Huck shook as he discovered his watch was gone. He had a sentimental attachment for that watch. He had won it from a Mexican gambler in a Texas border town two years previous, just a short time before that gambler had tried to shoot Huck because his senorita—the gambler's, not Huck's—had cast too many doe-eyed glances at the tall, black-haired, gray-eyed young Arizona cowhand.

The Mexican had lost his gun, as well as the watch, and a good slice of finger. This incident had cost Huck one .45 cartridge, the type to fit a long-barreled, single-action, blued-steel Colt sixgun with a wooden hand-carved grip worn smooth by much practice of the draw.

The senorita lost her interest in Huck, because he "try to keel my caballero," and Huck lost, in addition to the cartridge, some skin off his bronzed cheek, scraped off by the senorita's sharply pointed fingernails.

Yes, Huck had reason to prize that watch, but it was gone now. He had vague recollections of another poker game in connection with that watch, just the night before. A poker game which had taken place after he had had more drinks of Dishonest Abe Strealy's Take-a-Chance Saloon whiskey than go well with stud poker.

It appeared that the rest of the Bar X boys had vanished also. As Huck sat up in bed, staring about with eyes that cringed blearily against the glaring daylight, a clock outside chimed the hour of twelve. Each stroke was like a hammerblow on Huck's ringing head, causing the demon inside of it to give a spasmodic leap and land with all four feet. *Must* have four feet, Huck decided numbly. *Couldn't* raise all that hell with only two! Or maybe the demon walked on his hands as well as his feet.

As the clock boomed the last stroke of the hour, Huck interpreted the bright sunlight streaming through the window and decided it couldn't be midnight. That meant it was noon, if the clock knew what it was talking about, and clocks usually do. Which also meant that the bouncing caboose which was to haul the Bar X boys back to the Bar X ranch in Texas, west of the Pecos, had been on its way for some four hours.

In that caboose were Huck Brannon's "working" clothes—chaps, high-heeled boots, overalls, gunbelt, holsters, six-guns, and the rest of a fighting ranny's junk. All he had with him in this grubby rooming house were the clothes he stood in and that infernal headache.

It gradually dawned on Huck, somewhat tardily, that he would either have to walk to Texas or send a wire to Old Man Doyle, the

Bar X owner, for his fare. Even the rioting demon in his skull couldn't keep Huck from the instant decision that the second alternative was a forbidding one. And the first little better. . . .

He squirmed like a snake in a cactus patch at the thought of Old Man Doyle's raucous hoo-raws of laughter. Of the celestial amusement of Ah Sing, the Chinese cook, when Huck should arrive with his tail between his legs like a hound pup not old enough to take care of itself out of sight of its mammy.

He shifted uneasily, and the spring under the mattress groaned as he thought of Sue, Old Man Doyle's daughter. Sue wouldn't laugh at him—if he knew her at all, and hadn't he known her since she was knee-high to a jack-rabbit? Her clear amber eyes would smile at him and she would tell him in that rich, cool voice that it didn't matter—that being stranded in K.C. could happen to anyone. And she would laugh *with* him about it—not *at* him the way the rest would.

He squinted hard at the yellow stream of sun-light pouring in, conscious of a brand-new feel-ing of elation and well-being. The whiskey no longer bucked in his head. His square shoulders came up solidly. He tried to discover the source of this sudden tingling of satisfaction. It couldn't have been the last time he saw Sue. Or could it?

She'd been riding alongside him when he and the rest of the Bar X boys had pushed the herd

17

along to the terminal at Stevens Gulch where the long, crooked arm of the railroad bent its way to within twenty-five miles of the Bar X Ranch.

The morning had been still fresh and bright and new when they had started the herd up trail.

"Wait for me—wait for me, Huck," she had called, tearing after the cavvy and pulling up beside him. She sat her paint-pony as firmly and easily as any cowpoke. He remembered how the sun pushing its way over the crest of the far-off hills had cast a curious glow over Sue's face and struck dancing glints from her raven black hair.

"Mornin', Sue," he said, wheeling around to greet her. "What's the rush?"

"No rush, in particular," she said, suddenly confused. "I was just riding. Haven't I got a right to see Dad's cattle off to K.C.?"

"Shore—shore you have," he said, grinning at her, "but you'll scare the beef right off these steers rushin' up on 'em that way."

He was used to Sue riding alongside him. She had been doing it for a long time—out on the range, during roundups, combing the brake. And it was no different that morning, too, except— He didn't know. But there *was* a difference. In Sue. In himself.

"Darned if I see," he said, looking at her again, "how you manage to look so all-fired pretty this early in the mornin'."

Sue turned slowly and gave him a long slow look with those striking amber eyes. His look swept over her. She was tall and lithely graceful with sun-burnished skin that set off the perfect white teeth that showed in her rare, quick smiles. Right now, Huck could see the faint flush apparent beneath her bronze-stained cheeks.

She sighed. "Huck, sometimes I think you'll never stop treating me like a child."

Again he looked at her, long and deeply, aware of some curious, subtle change, some new stir within him—the surge of an undercurrent of feelings he didn't understand himself.

"Yeah," he said softly, the ghost of a smile playing around his lips. "You are kinda grown up. I guess I just didn't notice how much you'd growed. One minute you were a kid called Sue; and the next minute you're a grown up lady I have to call Miss Doyle." His soft voice was half serious, half mocking.

She dealt the mockery right back at him.

"That's right, Mr. Brannon," she said. "I think you should call me Miss Doyle." Then she suddenly burst into laughter. "And if you do, I'll have Dad run you right off the range."

And they laughed together; until a curious silence fell between them. But it wasn't like their old comradely silences. It was alive and charged. It was something they both felt, and both avoided mentioning.

"How long will the run take you, Huck?" she asked finally.

"Why, not more than three or four days."

"I'll miss you—you and the boys I mean, Huck."

"May be a little peaceful at that," he said. "But we'll be back before you know it."

The bawling cattle had finally been stowed in the cattle cars and Huck was passing the time of day with Sue. He remembered how cool her hand had been in his, and the soft look on her face.

"Take care of yourself, Sue," he said, "and don't forget which side to get on your hoss." It had sounded dull, wool-witted; not light and easy as he'd meant it to be. It had always gotten a rise out of her. But not this time.

"All right, Huck," she said slowly. "I won't forget. Don't stay too long, Huck."

Suddenly she had thrown her arms around his neck, pressed her lips to his, hard. Then she'd turned, vaulted into her saddle and was galloping away down the trail.

He had stood stock still for a moment, staring after her. Then as the train jerked into motion, he turned and vaulted into the slowly moving car.

Even now he could taste her lips on his. They —But what was he thinking about? He was only a waddy in her father's crew and a waddy with itching feet besides. What did he have to offer

Sue Doyle? Of course, Old Man Doyle did like him—No, it was crazy.

A horsefly buzzed around his head. He slapped at it absently and the movement brought him back to the dingy room with its ugly painted walls, its scarred and raddled furniture.

The dancing demon returned, but less malevolently than before.

The question now was, what to do? His room was paid for up to and including today, but half of today was already gone, and there was no provision for meals in his deal with the sour landlady, who had a baleful eye for six-foot cow-punchers with grin-wrinkles at the corners of their eyes and slight upward quirks at the corners of their wide, good-humored mouths.

He slapped cold water on his face, combed his hair and brushed off his clothes.

Outside, the white-golden sunshine and the autumn air, keen and crisp as old wine, was restorative. Suicide began to seem a project of unnecessary harshness. The dancing demon tired a little and Huck's head began feeling a trifle less like an over-stuffed melon.

A new complaint began to make itself felt, however. This time it was his stomach. Not, as in the case of his head, from what was in it; rather from what was not.

On the faint hope that the freight which was to carry the boys back to the Bar X might have been delayed, Huck headed for the railroad yards.

The train was gone, of course. The caboose had rolled out right on schedule, he learned from an unsympathetic yardmaster who had had more than one man's helping of trouble with cowtrains and cowpunchers and had scant use for either.

With a sigh, bitterly conscious of his empty pockets and emptier stomach, Huck sought a pile of railroad ties and perched disconsolately on them, running bronzed fingers through his short thick black hair, wondering among other things what had become of his broad-brimmed Stetson. Maybe it had gone with the watch in the poker game. And that sombrero had cost him forty good dollars new. He sighed again. The sigh brought results from an unexpected quarter:

"Feelin' sorta low, son?"

Huck glanced quickly around and saw nothing but what seemed to be more cross-ties. Then a somewhat thicker tie than the rest sort of heaved up at one end and showed a face—a face abandoned without signs of struggle to an untidy chaparral-thicket of hair and whiskers, out of which shone two twinkly eyes and a mess of wrinkles topped by a battered slouch hat.

The grin was contagious and, little as he felt like grinning right then, Huck could feel a response to it tugging at his own lips. "If I had the hat I ain't got, I could walk under a snake's belly and not touch a scale," he replied.

The little old man, sitting up, clucked sympathetically. "I know how you feel," he said, "I been there too. Sorta had a night of it last night, eh? Train go off and leave you?"

Huck nodded gloomily. The old man gave him a shrewd glance, cast a speculative eye toward a rickety little restaurant perched cheerfully on the embankment overlooking the railroad yards, and returned to Huck.

"Could you do with a cup of coffee 'bout now, son?"

In spite of his pride, Huck swallowed automatically and ran his tongue over his lips. The old man understood his moment of hesitation.

"I got the price," he chuckled. He raised a gnarled hand to cut off Huck's protest.

"Now don't go gettin' uppity, and figgerin' you don't wanta eat with a hobo. I done told you I been in yore boots 'fore now."

"It isn't that," Huck said. "It's just that I haven't a cent on me. And I can't stand my turn buyin'."

The old man chuckled again. "Want to know how you could return the favor?" he asked.

Huck nodded. "Sure."

"All right—do it this way. The next time you find some feller who's sorta up 'gainst it, you spend on him jest the same amount I spend on you t'day. Okay?"

Huck gave the little old man a long look from his level gray eyes. The look was returned, unflinchingly, from the blue eyes that had so much humor and savvy in their depths.

"Yes," said the cowboy quietly, "I'll do that; and thank you kindly."

Half an hour later, Huck Brannon heaved a deep sigh and reached for the makings. Tobacco and papers had in some way escaped last night's all-but-clean sweep, and he deftly rolled a cigarette with the slim fingers of his left hand, held it out to his table companion and manufactured one for himself.

"And now," said the old man, "I reckon the sensible thing to do will be to head you back toward Texas. I figger you haven't rode the rods or the blinds much, have you, son?"

Huck admitted he hadn't.

"If you had," continued the other, "I'd shove you onto the Limited which pulls out jest 'bout dark t'night; but that ain't no chore for a feller what ain't onto the ropes. A sidedoor Pullman is yore best bet, I callate. There'll be a manifest freight headin' in the gen'ral direction you'd oughta take in an hour or so. We'll mosey over to the yard and I'll point her out."

"You're not going in my direction?" Huck said regretfully.

"Nope, I got a little chore to do—somewheres else."

Huck noticed the slight hesitation on the old man's part. He let the question ride.

They talked on over several cigarettes, since they had until dusk before Huck could board the freight. The old-timer entertained with an unending stream of his adventures on the road, and Huck told a yarn or two about range-life. The remarks and questions the oldster asked showed he knew at least something about herding.

"You don't talk jest like the av'rage cowhand, son," he remarked as he rose from the table.

"I had a year in college," Huck told him. "Coupla bad years—blizzards, droughts—sorta set my dad back, and then his cayuse set his foot in a badgerhole one stormy night. The storm had started a stampede just before that, and— well, Dad and the bronc were in *front* of that stampede."

The old man clucked sympathetically and tactfully changed the subject.

"What'd you take in college?"

"Mining engineering," Huck replied. "Didn't do more than get started, though."

"Foller it up any since you left school?"

"Some—not as much as I wish I had. But you know how it is—range work sorta gets into a feller's blood, particular if you happen to be brought up to it—and you let other things slide. It's sorta contenting to have a good horse between your legs and a white moon up in the sky and the range rolling away toward the end of the world. . . ."

The old man nodded. "Uh-huh, jest 'nother form o' the 'open road.' Takes you 'way from the things sober-minded folks consider to be all what's wuth-while."

II

By Way of Colorado

They reached the railroad yards as the blue dusk was rolling over the prairie city like the wind-blown smoke from a thousand campfires. The old man quickened the pace as he sighted a long freight train standing up on a make-up track. Its headlight was gleaming, the blower was thundering and black smoke was pouring from the engine's stubby stack. The switchlight to the main lead glowed green.

"All ready to pull out," the old man muttered. "That's my train, son, we gotta hustle. C'mon, and I'll show you where yore rattler is corralled. She won't leave until after this westbound is outa the yards."

As they loped along beside the train, a big, hard-faced man suddenly stepped from between the cars. He had a rat-trap mouth and beady sullen eyes. His square, bulky body blocked their progress.

"Where you 'bo's think you're goin'?" he demanded in a voice that sounded like a sick bull's bellow.

The old man answered soothingly:

"Jest takin' a shortcut through the yards, officer. We—"

"Shortcut, hell!" the railroad detective snorted. He spat brown juice at their feet.

The old man started to speak again, but the bull lashed out with a vicious blow that caught him full in the mouth. The old man reeled back, clutching at the side of the boxcar for support.

"Get outa my yard, and stay out!" the bull roared. He drew back his fist a second time, and took a lumbering step forward.

With the smooth swiftness of a released spring, Huck Brannon went into action. He glided in front of the old man and blocked the railroad detective's swinging blow before it had travelled six inches. His left hand, balled into knuckles like iron knobs, came clear up from his knee. They smacked against the angle of the bull's jaw like a butcher's cleaver on a side of beef.

To the old 'bo, still dazed by the blow he had taken, it seemed as if the bull had suddenly sprouted wings. His feet left the ground and his blocky body rocketed through the air with all the grace of a cow gamboling with its calf. He hit the ground with a wallowing thud and his head snapped back against the projecting end of a crosstie. After a single twitching shudder he lay still, blood gushing from his lacerated scalp.

"G—good God, son, you've killed him!" the old man gasped.

"Reckon not," Huck said quietly. "Not with him bleeding like that."

He bent over the bull, thrust a sinewy hand under his coat and felt the solid thumping of a normally functioning heart.

"Can't kill his kind with anything short of a shovel or a pick handle," he growled, his gray eyes narrowing slightly as his groping hand contacted cold metal. "We'd better be moving before he gets his senses back enough to go for that hogleg he's wearing under his arm."

The old man's teeth chattered with apprehension. "They'll be another one close," he panted. "They allus work in pairs. We gotta get outa here 'fore they ketch us. It'll mean six months on the rock pile, if nothin' wuss."

His voice was suddenly drowned by the staccato notes of a whistle blowing two short ones, and the clangor of a locomotive's bell. The string of cars beside them creaked and groaned, there was a clang-jangle of couplings, a rattle of brake rigging. Then, from the far side of the slowly moving train, somebody shouted questioningly.

"That'll be his pardner," the old man whispered hoarsely. "He'll be comin' over here lookin' for him in a minute. C'mon, son, you gotta ketch this rattler with me. It ain't goin' the way you wanta head, but you'll get to Texas a damn sight faster by way of Colorado than by way of the K.C. jailhouse!"

Up at the head end of the long train the locomotive's stack belched black smoke and staccato thunder. The creaking of the wheels changed to a steady diapason of monotonous rumble. The boxcars swayed and rocked on their springs.

For a brief moment more Huck hesitated. All the things he would put behind him if he followed the oldtimer came crowding into his brain. The Bar X ranch, the laughing Chinaman, Ah Sing, his horse Smoke, Sue's last good-bye. His memory stuck on the last like a burr. He might be saying goodbye to all of them for a long, long time—perhaps forever. Why, maybe he'd never get back there—maybe he'd never see the old sights, the familiar faces—never see Sue again. That thought hurt like an old pain.

"Come on!" the old man croaked, shambling in unsteady steps beside the moving train. Huck was at his heels.

An instant later he gripped a grabiron with his bony hands and swung his foot onto the stirrup.

He vanished between the cars and Huck followed him, his sinewy body taking the leap with dynamic agility.

And at that instant a bulky figure floundered over a drawbar a couple of cars further back and thudded solidly to the ground. There was an instant of tingling suspense as Huck scrambled to reach the end-sill of the forward boxcar. Then—

Bang! bang! bang!

Huck ducked as the bullets whined past, smacking against the side boards, showering him with splinters. His right hand instinctively dropped to his thigh with effortless ease. He stifled a curse of dismay as his fingers encountered no gun. He peered quickly back along the train, and saw the bulky figure swing onto a grabiron with deceptive agility and come storming up the side of the car. A second later it vanished over the upper edge.

"He'll be on top of us in a minute," the cowboy muttered, "and that'll be the finish!"

Instantly Huck went into action, his brain working swiftly. "Outa here!" he barked, shuffling along the sill. "Outa here and up the embankment!"

"We won't have a chanct!" wailed the oldster. "That hellion up there'll see us go and if he don't plug us fust, he'll run us down."

"He'll get us for sure if we stay!" Huck shouted back. "C'mon, I tell you!"

He dropped from the slowly-moving train and the old man, still shrilling protests, followed him. Across the web of tracks Huck darted, reached the embankment and started clambering up it.

From the moving train sounded a yell of command. Spurts of flame lanced the darkness with orange streaks. The crackling of the gunshots sounded above the rumble of the train. Bullets fell like hail around them, churning through the cinders.

Huck heard the old man grunt, thought he might have been hit, and called out anxiously.

"Jest slipped on a rock," panted the oldtimer.

In another instant they were over the lip of the embankment. They dived into scrub which fringed the crest, burrowing deep behind the protecting brush. In one last backward glance, Huck had seen the railroad detective clambering down the car-side. Lights were bobbing about in the yard; questioning shouts came faintly to their ears.

"We can't get away, son," panted the old man. "They'll get dogs and run us down in the morning, even if they don't grab us t'night."

The cowboy was intent on watching the converging lights. He heard the bull shout instructions, caught a glimpse of his bulky form lumbering across the tracks.

"All right," he told the old man quietly,

"straight ahead—keep back outa sight. Straight ahead until we're 'round the bulge of the curve."

The old man, dominated by Huck's vigor and self-assurance, stifled his pessimistic plaints and followed Huck as he cut lithely through the growth. Before the detective had reached the lip of the embankment, the fugitives were around the bend. Below, they could see the boxcars filing heavily past as the long train gathered speed. For the moment they were out of sight of the pursuit.

Without a second's hesitation, Huck went sliding down the embankment toward the tracks. The old man, understanding his purpose at last, grunted approval. He followed close behind Huck and they reached the moving train together.

"Look!" he exclaimed. "Here comes a empty— door half open! Think we can make it?"

"Easy," replied Huck coolly, running along beside the rocking boxcars.

Along came the empty, its wheels drumming hollowly. With one hand Huck caught the door jamb, and rested his other lightly on the sill. With a leap and a scramble, he was inside the car. Turning swiftly he reached down a hand to his companion. The old man gripped it and the big cowboy lifted him into the car with no apparent effort.

Together they crouched on the rough boards,

peering through the opening, listening for sounds of pursuit. On the embankment they could see lanterns winking about like angry fireflies, vanishing one by one as the pursuers beat their way deeper into the brush.

"Godfrey, feller, but you're smart!" exclaimed the old man, "making them hellions think we was cuttin' 'crost country and then doublin' back onto the train again. All we got to do now is watch the big yards over to Washoe on the chanct that they telegraph ahead to search the train for us there, which I don't figger they'll do. Yeah, we're settin' purty now."

He leaped to his feet and ducked as a voice suddenly spoke over his shoulder.

"Yeah, that's the idea, brother. Come back where it's comf't'ble, and set!"

III

Al Fresco Breakfast

Huck took a long step, hugging the inner wall of the car. The voice sounded friendly enough, but he was taking no chances.

"Just who are you, feller?" he asked, and instantly shifted his position again.

A single chuckle sounded in the dark, followed by a pair of others.

"Jest three titled gents," replied the voice, "lords of leisure—knights of the road. We heard the shin-dig and cal'lated somebody's got in bad with the yard dicks. Glad to see you out-smarted the lousy loafers. Wait a minute—till we're clear of the yards—and I'll make a light. We got a lantern here and there's plenty of straw in this end of the car. Keep outa t'other end—there's firebrick loaded there. Reckon that's how this door didn't happen to be sealed —nobody's gonna carry off firebrick. Figger it's bound for the Colorado smelters or stamp mills, mebbe."

Silence followed for a space. Then a match scratched and a tiny flame flickered. It was suc-ceeded by the warm, steady glow of a lantern in whose light Huck could distinguish three grin-ning faces crowned by unbelievably tattered hats. A scrub of beard covered each face; but the eyes of all were unanimously good-humored and friendly.

One man was wondrously obese, the other two as magnificently scrawny. The fat man waved a hand to the straw heaps.

"Draw up, brothers, and set," he invited them.

Grinning, Huck and the old man obeyed, set-tling themselves comfortably in the straw. The click of the wheels over the rail joints was quickening its tempo, the car was beginning to lurch and sway.

"Name's Mason—Lank Mason," the fat man offered. "This here scantlin' on my right is Fatty Bromes; one on the left is Bad-eye Wilson: they're headin' for Californy. Colorado's my stop— Apishapa River country in Las Animas County."

Huck saw his friend give a slight start and bend shrewd eyes on Mason. But he said nothing beyond announcing his own name.

"Gaylord," he said, "Tom Gaylord. Most folks call me Old Tom, which is short and easy and saves wear and tear on the tongue."

The others nodded and Huck introduced himself.

"Now everybody knows everybody else, we jest might as well take it easy," said Mason. "Stretch out and be comf'table, only watch out for the lantern. Don't wanta start a fire in this straw. Car of blastin' powder right ahead of us and that stuff goes off mighty sudden and mighty hard if you tetch a light to it. So be keerful of yore smokes, too."

He began tamping a blackened pipe with stubby paws. Huck noticed how powerful the fingers were that manipulated the tobacco. "Thought you said you were a gent of leisure?" he remarked, offhand.

The fat man chuckled. "How do you know I ain't?" he countered.

Huck gestured at the roughened, calloused fingers. "Your hands never got that way from settin' on 'em," he replied.

The other nodded. "You got sharp eyes, son, the kind what don't miss much. Nope, I don't do over-much loafin', even though I am takin' it easy right now. Fact is, the reason I'm on this rattler is 'cause I'm headin' for what oughta be a new job, and money comes too hard to spend on railroad tickets when you can be jest as comf'table in a side-door Pullman for free. I'm headin' for the new Esmeralda gold diggin's. I'm a hard-rock man mostly, but I know somethin' 'bout hydraulic minin', and that's what they're usin' over there. They're knockin' down a hull mountainside of gravel and doin' purty well at it, I hear tell. Payin' good wages, anyhow."

Again Huck saw old Tom Gaylord's eyes gleam with interest, but again the oldster held his tongue. Huck wondered exactly what cards the old man was playing so close to his skinny chest.

All night long the freight roared across the plains of Kansas. Lulled by the steadily clicking wheels and the monotonous rumble of the cars, Huck Brannon slept the profound sleep of untroubled youth. But still it was a catlike sleep. Each time the train slowed to a stop at lonely pumping stations for water or fuel, the cowboy drifted awake to the changing tempo of sound and movement. He'd never law-dodged before, and it made him jumpy.

It was the grunting and stirring of fat Lank Mason which fully and finally aroused him in the gray dawn. He sat up, brushing the straw from his rumpled black hair, and grinned sleepily at the fat man. Lank grinned back, shook himself like a big dog coming out of the water, and began burrowing under the straw heaped along the wall. He drew forth a gunny sack that clanked as he shook it. From the sack he took an array of tin cans that had not yet known the ravaging touch of a can opener.

"Breakfast in the dining car—right here—in fifteen minutes," Lank observed, hauling out a flat slab of sheet iron from beneath another straw heap.

He laid the slab of tin near the partly open car door, cupped up the edges and criss-crossed some splinters of wood on its surface. Then he went after the cans with a huge jacknife, ripping them open, flattening some of them after pouring out the contents, which he carefully heaped on the flattened sheets when they were ready. Then he struck a match to the splinters of wood, which burned with a brisk and almost smokeless flame.

"Allus pick yore wood for fire and no smoke," he observed to the interested cowboy.

Over the flame and glowing embers he whisked the homemade "skillets," deftly turning the contents with the blade of the jackknife.

In almost no time at all smoking hot sausages, savory strips of fried bacon and slabs of steaming corned beef were ready for eating.

One of the hoboes came lugging a can of water from a corner of the car. More wood was placed on the glowing sheet iron and coffee brewed swiftly in the can.

"I've seen some mighty smart cooking out on the range," Huck observed, "but this beats anything I ever ran into."

After they'd eaten all their belts could hold comfortably, they lit up pipes and cigarettes and smoked in dreamy comfort, staring out of the open door at the corn and wheat fields, the stretches of rolling grassland that flew past in endless panorama of sun-drenched peace.

"We'll hit the Washoe yards in a hour or so now," Old Tom observed.

"Yeah," nodded Lank. "Hafta unload then. There's an alley 'longside the yard lead, jest 'fore they stop to change engines. We'll duck inter that and lie low until she's ready to pull out again. Think they'll be lookin' for you two fellers?"

"Don't think so," Gaylord replied. "Got a notion this quick-thinkin' young hellion fooled 'em proper. Chances are they're still beatin' up the brush or combin' the town for us."

"Sounds reasonable," admitted Lank. "I got a notion it'll work out jest as you figger."

It did. They passed the Washoe yards without incident, leaving the train in case of an inspection by the bulls, lying in the long grass of the alley until the wheels began to turn again and then making a quick dash for the open car.

All day the train boomed across endless plains, the grade climbing steadily; and as the dusk began to turn the hollows into mystic blue lakes of shadow, the skyline changed. Ahead were vast, nebulous shapes rising into the sun-washed vault. Shadowy and unreal at first, they swiftly took on solidity and form.

"Mountains," Old Tom grunted. "We're in Colorado, now, shootin' through Baco County. Las Animas next, and my stop."

"Mine, too," Lank Mason remarked, "over near the Huerfano line."

The train roared into a cut, crashed through between steeply restraining walls, and then thundered along in the deepening shadow of towering cliffs.

Huck leaned against the jamb of the boxcar door and rested his eyes wonderingly on the wild grandeur of the mountain scenery looming against the angry red of a stormy sunset sky. It was Huck who—even before the engineer of the manifest—first saw the avalanche of earth and stone roaring down toward the track over which the train would have to pass.

Under the beat of winter hail and summer rain,

that gaunt cliff had stood throughout the ages—had staunchly resisted the onslaught of the elements. But the patient, never resting, never despairing fingers of frost and water probed deeper and deeper, prying strata from strata, cracking with quiet, persistent strength the heart of eternal rock itself.

And now, the air waves disturbed by the pounding exhaust of the giant locomotive provided the final kinetic push necessary to disturb the delicate balance of the hesitating granite.

Outward and downward, slowly, majestically at first, as if reluctant to leave its bed of the eons, the mighty mass answered the resistless pull of gravity. With appalling swiftness it gathered speed, rolling, tumbling, with individual segments the size of a house leaping high into the air and hurtling through space for hundreds of yards.

Like the raised lip of an angry dog, the grinding flood upreared at the edge of the towering battlement that flanked the right-of-way. It seemed to poise for a moment, straining for greater height in its upward sweep; then the curling lip broke raggedly and hurtled downward toward the slim wisps of the tracks half a thousand feet below.

IV

Roaring Death

In the locomotive cab, the grizzled engineer, a veteran of half a dozen wrecks in the wild mountain country, fought with every trick he knew to save his train from that mighty surge. His fireman's warning yell had been his first inkling of disaster ahead as the engine lurched around a curve. He slammed the throttle shut and threw on every ounce of pressure in his brake cylinders.

The screech of air through the port, the clanging of brake rigging and the grind of the shoes against the wheels added their pandemonium to the tumult of the avalanche. Back came the reverse lever, the old hogger jerked the throttle wide open.

The exhaust boomed again and the great drive wheels, working in reverse, howled their protest and ground flakes and ribbons of steel from the shivering rails. Back along the train clattered a prodigious banging of couplers and clanging of outraged steel.

But it was useless. The terrific shove of ten

million pounds of freight traveling at sixty miles an hour hurled the train forward despite the grip of the brakes and the backward surge of the giant engine. With a prodigious crash the locomotive hit the towering wall of earth and stone, burrowing deep into the mass, thrown over on its side. Down upon the hissing monster thundered tons of rock from the wavering crest.

The engineer died with one hand on the throttle, the other on the brake-valve lever. The fireman, jumping through the window an instant before the crash, was crushed to a pulp under the roaring mass of the avalanche. The head brakeman met death in the crushed cab, pinned against the hot boilerhead, screaming his agony as life was baked out of him. Jets of smoke and steam spurted through the crevices of the ghastly mound and wavered above the sullen funeral pyre like uncertain ghosts in the fading light.

The wreck was appallingly complete. Car after car left the iron to slide and roll down the steep slope on the off side of the right-of-way. Others piled up in a jumbled mass of splintered wood and twisted steel. Still others were turned sideways or lay with tangled brake rigging in the air. Everywhere were trucks torn loose from the bodies, beams, sills, scattered freight.

And hardly had the last screech of disrupted steel and the final grumble of the avalanche ceased to quiver on the air when, back toward the middle of the shattered train, an ominous glow began to redden the deepening dusk.

Huck Brannon had hardly time to yell a warning to his companions when he was thrown to the floor by the bucking of the car as the engineer slammed the automatic brake lever into the "big hole" and "dynamited" his train. He was still rolling about in the straw when the engine hit the slide.

Gripping, clawing, vainly trying to gain his feet, he was hurled against the side of the car with terrific force. Over and about him rained the heavy firebrick. One grazed his forehead and for a crawling moment or two, everything went black.

He was dimly conscious of a mighty crashing and splintering and the horrible grinding groan of the overturned cars slithering down the slope. Vaguely aware, also, of yells and screams close at hand.

It was Mason's booming voice that shook Huck back into full consciousness. His voice and the pound and scuffle of his brogans. Sick and dizzy, Huck reeled to a stance on a slanting surface. He coughed as something acrid and penetrating struck his throat and nostrils. Shaking the red-streaked blackness from his eyes he glared about.

The boxcar was ripped apart, unroofed, splintered. Overhead Huck saw the glint of stars in the darkening sky. All about him was swirling smoke through which beat a rising glow. Against the glow leaped and danced a huge figure.

The figure whirled suddenly and Huck saw it was Lank Mason. The big miner saw him at the same instant.

"Didn't get you either, eh?" he shouted. " 'Fraid the rest of the boys are done for. Here's Badeye with his head bashed in and Fatty's damn nigh tore in two. Where's the old man? We gotta get outa here pronto—that lantern smashed and set the straw afire. These splinters have caught, too. I tried to beat it out, but ain't no use."

At mention of Old Tom, Huck recollected the queer gasping sound which could still be heard. It seemed to come from beneath what remained of one side of the smashed car. With Lank at his heels, he crawled over the wreckage in the direction of the sound.

Ripping the shattered planks away, they found Old Tom. He lay buried deep in the wreckage; a heavy beam, resting across his chest, pinned him down. One end of the beam was securely bolted to the long double timbers of a side sill. Upon the other end lay the huge steel center sill, a dead weight of more than a ton.

Gaylord was conscious and, it seemed to Huck, not fatally injured. The weight upon his chest made breathing very nearly impossible, and he was in pain, but the beam was so supported by the wreckage that it did not badly crush him.

Old Tom recognized them and gasped out words of satisfaction on their escape.

"We'll get you out, oldtimer," Huck assured him. "Is it hurting bad? Can you hold out while we get that damned sill off or until the wreck-train gets here?"

"Ain't hurt bad," panted Gaylord. "Weight don't seem to be settlin' no more. I can wait."

"You can't wait long," growled Lank. "Fire's eatin' this way, and there ain't no way we can put it out. C'mon, young feller, let's get to work on that sill."

They went after it, heaving and tugging. The sill did not budge an inch. Mason swore and mopped his beefy face. Huck ripped free a length of timber for them to use as a pry. Still the sill stubbornly held its ground. Again they put their strength to the effort. The veins stood out on Huck's forehead large as cords, black as ink. The big muscles of arm and back and shoulder swelled and knotted beneath his shirt. With a slithery sound, one sleeve split from elbow to wrist.

"Gawd, feller, but you got an arm on you!" panted Lank Mason. "I allus been rated a hoss, but I figger you as liftin' half again as much as I am."

"But not enough, blast it!" Brannon grated behind set teeth. "Mason, we've got to do something and damn fast or he's a goner sure."

"Fire won't reach him for quite a spell," Lank said. "See—it's workin' t'other way. Wind's blowin' in that d'rection, and most of the wood's over there."

"Yeah, and something else is over there, too," Huck told him grimly.

"Eh?"

"Uh-huh, that car of blasting powder's over that way, and the fire's all over it right now. Any minute, she's liable to let go."

"Good Gawd!" the miner gasped. "When she does she'll blow this mess clean to Utah!"

"And Old Tom with it—if we don't get him out first," Huck said quietly.

Growling, Lank leaped to the pry and bent his great shoulder to it. Then he suddenly straightened up, staring back along the wreck; a light was bobbing toward them from that direction.

"Here comes one of the train crew," he muttered. "Mebbe he can help."

A moment later the conductor of the freight came stumbling over the ties. There was blood on his face and one of his eyes was swelled shut. He paused opposite the burning wreckage and glared at the pair with the one eye remaining open, as if they were responsible for the wreck.

"What the hell's goin' on *here?*" he demanded.

Huck told him briefly. Before he had finished,

the conductor was slipping and sliding down the embankment. His practiced eye took in the situation at once.

"Gotta get that feller out in a hurry if he's to be got out at all," he declared. "Here, all t'gether now!"

He bent his back to the pry and the three tugged and strained until their faces were black.

"No use," the conductor grunted. "We ain't got the heft."

He coughed spasmodically as acrid smoke swirled about them in thick clouds.

"Thank God the wind's changed," he gulped. "That'll keep the fire 'way from that powder a little while longer."

"And bring it onto Old Tom a little sooner," Huck pointed out.

"What in hell we gonna do?" Lank Mason wailed helplessly.

Huck Brannon's gray eyes were roving over the wreckage lighted by the blazing wood. His gaze ran up the embankment, centered on the shining rails still securely spiked to the crossties, came back to the massive steel sill which held Old Tom prisoner. He estimated the distance, a deep furrow of concentration drawing his dark brows together.

Long-neglected engineering elementals were coming back to him. He groped in his mind, try-ing to pin down an elusive memory, a memory that dealt with heavy timbers on an incline—timbers that were needed higher up the slope at a time when there was no windlass or hoist available, and insufficient man-power to move them by hand.

"We got those logs up, though," he muttered. "Let's see, now, there was a tree growing on top of the rise. We had—"

Suddenly he whirled to face the conductor, his eyes blazing with excitement.

"You got rope in your caboose?" he demanded.

"Shore," the railroad man replied, "nigh onto a hundred feet of stout cord in the forward cushion box—chains, too; but what good'll that do? Can't pull that sill off with rope."

"I'll show you," the cowboy barked, and scrambled up the slope.

"I gotta hustle to the head end and see what happened to the boys there," the conductor bawled after him. "The rear man's gone back to flag the Western Flyer. She'll have telegraph instruments and can cut in on the wire and call the wrecker."

V

Spanish Windlass

Huck waved a hand to show he understood, and headed for the caboose at a dead run. He found it sagging crazily to one side, the front wheels off the track and its coupling twisted loose. He leaped up the steps, into the aisle and flung back the cushion seat that was hinged to the box.

The rope was there, neatly coiled. Huck hauled it out, shouldered it and staggered down the steps. It was a heavy weight and it was rough going through the dark; but he made almost as good time back to the burning wreckage as he had coming from it. He could see the conductor's lantern bobbing about the dark mass of the avalanche; but Lank Mason still crouched beside Gaylord, coughing and choking in the smoke.

"Gettin' hotter'n hell," he panted as Huck came sliding down the embankment.

"That powder car's blazin' fine, too," the cowboy grunted. "She'll go any minute now."

With swift, sure hands he looped one end of the rope about the steel sill.

"Get two strong beams, ten or twelve feet long," he shouted back at Mason as he clambered up the slope again, trailing the rope.

To reach the track and secure the free end of the rope to the outside rail took only minutes. The rope sagged down the slope with plenty of slack.

Huck found a spot halfway down the slope where a large flat stone provided secure footing.

"Bring those beams up here," he called to Lank.

The miner panted up with them, mumbling questions which Huck didn't have time to answer. He handed one to the cowboy, who stood the unsplintered end on the flat rock, thrusting the splintered end through a loop twisted in the slack of the rope.

"Hold it," he grunted, took the other timber and thrust one end through the widened loop.

With Lank holding the upright beam steady, Huck gripped the far end of the horizontal beam and walked around the upright, winding the slack of the rope about the vertical beam. And now he had a crude Spanish windlass capable of exerting a tremendous pull on the sill that penned Old Tom.

"If the rope'll hold, we'll do it," he told Mason. "You come and take the end of this—the upright will stand by itself now the rope's taut. Wind her up slow and steady and pull the sill up the slope.

I'm going to jerk Tom out soon as the weight's off him."

"If that powder let's go, you won't have a chance!" warned Mason. "Let *me* go down, son."

"I'm faster on my feet and stronger," Huck replied. "You're better here. All right, steady, now."

Swiftly he lunged back into the inferno of smoke and fire. The rope hummed with tension and as Huck crouched beside Old Tom, the heavy steel sill began to slowly move up the sloping timber. As it moved, the lower end of the timber and the wreckage to which it was bolted raised slightly, easing the pressure on Gaylord's chest.

The old man opened his eyes, coughed, shuddered, stared dazedly about him. His glance centered on the cowboy crouched beside him, shielding him with his own body from the withering heat of the fire which crept nearer and nearer. Understanding brightened his pain-glazed eyes.

"Get out, son," he croaked. "Get out and leave me—it ain't no use—that powder's due to let go—get out and save yoreself while you can."

Huck Brannon, his hair crisping and the clothes on his back smoking from the heat, grinned painfully.

"Go to hell, you old loafer," he gasped. "Who's doin' this, anyhow?"

With a moan, Old Tom fainted again. Huck

crouched lower, hands ready to grip the beam the instant the sill lifted.

He could hear Lank Mason grunting and cursing above the roar of the flames. A distant shout sounded as the conductor came stumbling back up the track. With a crash a whole side of the powder car fell away. Huck could see the squat containers and the tongues of fire reaching toward them. Stinging sparks showered his uncovered head. The smoke rolled about him in hot, choking clouds.

He blinked his streaming eyes and strained ears that were now beginning to ring queerly. He could no longer see the moving sill and pitched his hearing to the crunching that would denote its passage from the beam to the rubble of the embankment.

Through a haze of pain he heard it, felt the sudden upward spring of the beam. He gripped the rough wood with blistered hands, felt the seared skin sluff off in a mist of white agony. With every atom of his sinewy strength he heaved at the beam, lifting till his sinews cracked and his swelling muscles threatened to crush his bones.

The beam creaked, groaned, resisted stubbornly, then gave with a rush. Huck hurled it aside, stooped over Old Tom Gaylord and lifted his limp body. He could hear Lank shouting anxiously. From the tracks above came the conductor's warning bellow. Huck reeled about and staggered painfully up the embankment.

"Hightail, you fellers!" he shouted hoarsely, "she's gonna let go! Hightail, you can't help me —you'll jest get in my way!"

Cursing insanely, they obeyed him. Lank topped the rise and pounded after the conductor. Flaming timbers fell full upon the powder containers as the end of the car gave way. The fire roared its triumph. Miles above him, dancing in a welter of smoke and agony, Huck could make out the lip of the embankment and the shining rails.

He strained toward it, reeling drunkenly, the slight body of Old Tom Gaylord an increasing weight with every wavering step. He slipped, fell to one knee and flung out a hand that touched the cold steel of the outer rail. He gripped the iron, drew himself over the lip, reeled erect and lurched down the track. A dozen frenzied strides, a score, twice a score—

Behind him there was a mighty fluff of bluish smoke, a red blaze that paled the shrinking stars, a roar like the rending of creations. The mighty concussion flung the cowboy and the man he carried as by the thrust of a giant hand. He reeled, scrambled, tried to keep his balance, and plunged headlong. Dazzling white light blazed before his eyes as he struck the rough ties, then wave on wave of pain-streaked blackness hurled him into bottomless depths of chilling cold.

Huck Brannon awoke with his aching head on a pillow and his pain-racked body in a comfortable bunk. To his ears came a clanging and crashing and hissing interspersed by a metallic chattering and the shouts of men.

For a moment he lay staring up at a low, boarded ceiling. He sniffed the smell of boiling coffee and food cooking and realized that in spite of the pain that racked him, he was terrifically hungry. With a vast effort he turned his head—and looked straight into the face of an impressive-looking man he couldn't remember ever having seen, who gazed down at him from a pair of frosty blue eyes of amazing keenness.

Their owner was well above middle height and massively and robustly built. His shoulders were of great breadth, his arms long and powerful. He had a craggy eagle's beak of a nose above a wide, tightly clamped mouth whose sternness was relieved by the numerous quirkings of the corners. A snowy bush of crinkly white hair frizzed back from a dome-shaped forehead. He nodded to Huck and spoke to him in a deep and resonant voice.

"Hmm! Decided to come out of it at last, eh? How you feel?"

"About as if I'd been dragged through a knothole and then hung on a barbed wire fence to dry," Huck admitted. "Otherwise not so bad. Everything seems to be in working order." He

54

gingerly flexed his arms and legs and swiveled his head from side to side.

The big oldster grunted. "You're lucky," he said. "There were rocks and chunks of iron and big timbers piled all over the place where we found you. When you were knocked down, you sort rolled under the bulge of the cliff. Reckon that saved you."

Huck sat up abruptly, despite the protests of a brand-new set of pains that his sudden movement stabbed through him.

"Old Tom—Old Tom Gaylord"—he panted, fighting the nausea that crawled around the pit of his stomach—"did he—"

"You can't kill a hobo," the old man growled. "He's in the bunk up ahead of you with a couple of broken ribs and a badly bruised chest and back. Keep him laid up for a month or two, I guess. He owes you his life. I heard the whole story from the freight conductor and that miner-fellow."

Huck sank back onto his pillow, much relieved. The old man gazed at him with those canny eyes.

"Where you heading, son?" he asked.

"The mines over to Esmeralda," Huck replied, remembering Lank Mason's destination. "Expect to find work there," he added, recalling abruptly that the lantern used by himself and his companions was responsible for the fire and subsequent explosion.

The old man might be a member of the railroad police and as such would doubtless act harshly toward wandering knights of the road with no legitimate destination in view. Honest workmen in search of employment he might regard in a less gloomy light.

The old man's gaze fixed upon Huck's sinewy right hand, the burns grease-smeared, which lay palm upward upon the rough blanket.

"Those callouses don't look like the kind that come from a pick and shovel," he remarked dryly, adding with meaning, "particularly those on the thumb and first finger."

Huck's gray eyes met the cold blue ones steadily.

"I haven't anything to hide," he said quietly. "Yeah, those across the palm were made by a grass rope, and that one on the thumb—well, because a man practices the draw doesn't necessarily mean he's a cow-thief or a dry-gulcher."

"Not necessarily," the old man agreed, "even if it is mighty unusual to find a cowboy riding a manifest freight and heading for a mining camp. Well, that's your business, and what you did to save that old fellow was commendable—and smart."

"Where am I—and where's Lank?" Huck asked.

"You are in a wreck-train bunk-car," the old man replied. "And the big miner—that's Lank, I guess—is helping the crew clean up the mess.

"We'll be rolling in about half an hour, now," he added, "and this outfit is headed for Esmeralda, the mining town. If you decide to stay there for a spell and—work, you might drop in and see me when I come back this way next month."

Before Huck could form a question, the old man turned and passed through the end door of the car.

A moment later a capped and aproned Negro stuck a shining black face through the doorway and flashed a dazzling set of ivories at the cowboy.

"Howdy, boss, and how you feelin'?" he said. "Figurate you could do with a right smart helpin' of po'k chops and fried 'taters 'bout now. Like to hab me bring the vittles in here to you?"

"I can make it to the table, thanks just the same," Huck told him, swinging his feet stiffly to the floor and reaching for his clothes, which lay neatly folded on a nearby bench.

The darky grinned and bobbed his head.

"By the way," Huck called as he turned back to the cook car, "who was the big feller who was talking to me just now?"

"Dat was de *big* feller, for sho'," grinned the darky. "Dat gen'man was nobody else but Mistuh Jaggers Dunn, de gen'ral manager of dis whole railroad."

"Jaggers Dunn?"

"Yassuh, dat's what de boys call him when he

ain't 'round—Jaggers—Mistuh James G. Dunn is de sorta uppity proper way of his namin', I perspaculate. He jest headed back to his private car, de *Winona*, what's hooked onter de rear end of de Western Flyer standin' in back of us. Ol' Flyer's 'bout ready to pull out, now de track is cleaned up again. Yeah, dere she comes now, whackety-whack-in' past de sidin'. We all will be headin' for Esmeralda soon as she clears."

However, two long coal drags rumbled past before the wreck train was given a clear block.

"They're switchin' them strings of black diamonds in front of the second section of the Western Flyer," the wreck train foreman remarked to Huck. "That will delay the second section still more, but it can't be helped. Coal is mighty important on this division—can't take a chance on the supply gettin' too low. Have to haul it a long ways to Esmeralda—that's a division point for the C. & P., you know—and the big yards and shops are there."

"Must be mighty expensive, making a long haul like that," the cowboy observed.

"It is," said the foreman, "but they ain't nothin' to do 'bout it. No mines in this district, and you gotta have fuel to keep a railroad goin'. Coal bill for the Mountain Division is jest 'bout double, mebbe more, what it costs on any other division. There she clears, and old Sam's tootin' two shorts. All 'board for Esmeralda, gents!"

VI

Sue Doyle

The Bar X Ranch stood strategically in the center of a wide, sweeping valley. To the north and south as far as the eye could see, rolled rich and luxurious grassland, with heavy gramma grass reaching belly-high to a good-sized horse. Cotton-woods, cool and inviting in the warm autumn sun, dotted the range.

To the east and west, hills rose gently to mark the outer boundaries of this pleasant, sun-warmed valley. A broad leisurely stream stemmed out of the upper reaches of the northern slopes, feeding the soil with its watery richness.

Large herds of cattle watched by lazy-riding cowboys grazed and wandered along the banks of the meandering stream. The cattle were fat and sleek and content.

Sue Doyle, in the midst of all this rich contentment and serenity, felt its gnawing contrast to her own state of mind. For a long time she had been lying on her back in the shade of a large elm tree that stood directly in front of the low, rambling ranchhouse. She stared moodily and sightlessly up through the leaves to the opaque blue of the Texas sky; her mouth was drawn in a fretful line and her slender fingers drummed nervously on the turf.

Suddenly a shadow fell across her line of vision. For an instant it was only a patch of darkness. Then it took shape.

"Dad!" she cried, suddenly agitated, and rose to her feet with inexplicable speed. In fact, she behaved just as she had, as a child, when she'd been caught trying to roll a cigarette behind the barn. "I didn't see you."

"I reckon you didn't," said her father.

Old Man Doyle, as he was called by all who knew him, including his hired hands, was short, thin and wiry; his hair was scraggly, with patches of red, sun-frazzled scalp showing through where the hair was thinning. The patches were hidden now, by an old, battered Stetson that crowned his top.

From under its misshapen brim stared two mildly inquisitive brown eyes, between which ran a short, decisive nose whose end exploded into a bright red bulb. The mouth was long and wide, and was shaped for loud and raucous laughter.

For a small man, his voice was deep and resonant. His talk seemed to rumble up out of his belly rather than from his vocal chords.

"I didn't see you," Sue repeated, stupidly. She

was a head taller than her father and looked down upon him with a curiously disturbed glance.

He looked at her shrewdly for a moment and cocked his head on a side. "Yuh ain't been seein' *anythin'* lately," he said good-naturedly. Then his tone grew more earnest. "What's troublin' yuh, lass? Yuh ain't been yourself for a couple weeks now—ever since the boys come back from K.C. What's eatin' yuh?"

"Nothing," she replied quickly. Almost too quickly. "I'm restless, I guess."

"Yeah," said Old Man Doyle, eyeing her steadily. Her gaze dropped under his. "I reckon I ain't much of a ma to yuh, Sue. Been a mite easier if she'd of been here for yuh to talk to. Ma's are a sight better'n easier to talk to than pa's, I reckon."

Sue's white teeth showed in a smile. Impulsively she flung her arms around his neck and kissed him. For a moment they grinned at each other self-consciously.

"You've been both to me, Dad," she said. Then her tone deepened as her eye fell on a big blue-horse, cropping grass in the courtyard. "Do you think anything's happened to Huck?"

Doyle's eye followed her gaze. She was staring at Huck Brannon's Smoke. His brow corrugated in a wrinkle, then smoothed out. When he spoke, his tone was casual, hearty and innocent.

"To Huck Brannon?" he cried. "Nothin' could happen to that young hellion."

"Then why hasn't he come back? Why didn't he return with the rest of the boys?"

"Why, they told yuh, Sue," replied her father, his eyes peering keenly at her from beneath his battered hat. "He had a coupla drinks too many an' jest forgot to get up the next mornin'; an' the boys said he was plumb busted. I reckon he kinda got stranded in K.C."

"But why didn't he wire for money to come back?"

"I figger he wouldn't want to do that, daughter. You know Huck."

"Then where is he now?"

"I cal'late he's hoofin' it back, Sue—that is— if he aims to come back atall."

The blood ebbed slowly from the girl's face. Her eyes widened to deep, amber pools. "What do you mean, Dad?"

"I mean, mebbe he's left the Bar X for good. He always said he'd wander on, some fine day."

For a moment the only sound in the afternoon was the far-off tinkle of a horse's bell. "Yes, I know," Sue said. "Only—no, it just isn't possible!"

"How do yuh know, daughter?"

"I do know it," she replied quickly. She couldn't tell her father about kissing Huck. Not when it might look as if Huck was staying away because of it. She pointed to Smoke instead.

"Huck's horse is here. He'd never leave his horse. Besides, his clothes are here too—and his guns."

"Is that all?" he asked.

"Yes," she replied hesitantly.

"Wal, I reckon a hombre can get other clothes an' buy another hoss."

"No, no," she insisted. "Huck wouldn't go away without—I'm sure something must have happened to him! I'm sure of it! We'd have heard something by now."

Doyle surveyed his daughter, from the tips of her small booted feet to the crest of her thick, wavy black hair. She colored under his penetrating gaze, but her eyes held firm.

"Wal," he drawled, " 'pears to me that yuh been mighty concerned over that cowboy since he ain't come back." He hesitated a moment, then, "Don't tell me yuh've gone soft on Huck, Sue?"

It was a question that demanded an answer. For a moment, her glance held steady, then it faltered. "I don't know, Dad. I honestly don't know." She looked up into his face again. "I guess I sort of got used to riding with him and being with him—I don't know, Dad. All I know is that I'm lonely when Huck's not around. And so I miss him."

"An' how does this here cowboy feel 'bout yuh, daughter?"

She laughed aloud, tossing her head. "I don't know."

"See here, Sue," he cried indignantly. "I ain't gonna have a daughter of mine throwin' herself into the arms of the first good-lookin' rapscallion that sets foot in a stirrup."

"I'm not throwing myself at anybody, Dad," she assured him quietly.

"Then what are yuh aimin' to do?"

"I'm going to Kansas City to look for him. I think something has happened to him."

He was on the point of raising an objection, but one look at the determination written bright and steady in his daughter's face, changed his mind.

"Yuh always was a stubborn monkey!" he exclaimed. There was a hint of admiration in his voice, as well as love for this headstrong daughter of his. Then a thought struck him.

"Why don't yuh let me send one of the boys first, to look for him? If he's in trouble maybe he'll need more help than a girl can give him." She looked hesitant. "Ain't no use yuh're chasin' after him, when I can send Lem or Jim. Is there?"

She shook her head again.

"No, Dad," she said. "I've got to go myself. If something's happened to Huck—I want to be there."

He tried one last appeal.

"A'right, Sue," he said. "But why not wait a couple of days more? Mebbe yore Huck Brannon will turn up by his own self."

"I'll wait two days—but if Huck doesn't return—I'm going to look for him." And there was no hesitation at all on her face or in her voice.

VII

Salty Town

Esmeralda! Division point for the great C. & P. railroad, whose fingers of steel were reaching through the mountains toward the far-off Pacific. As yet, the great yellow passenger trains and the rumbling freights had to use a leased line to reach the western coast; but the dream of Jaggers Dunn, ex-cowboy, miner, engineer, division-superintendent—now empire builder, guiding genius of the great trunk line—the dream of a network of steel from the gray Atlantic to the blue waters of the "Peaceful Ocean," from the pines of Canada to the palms of the Gulf, was at last coming true.

Here at Esmeralda was his newest outpost. Here on the grim mountain frontier, where the law of knife and gun was still the ruling law. Where blood and passions ran crimson-bright in the veins of strong-limbed, lusty men, glorious in their recklessness; gallant in their disregard for hardship and personal danger; superb in their thirst for adventure and achievement, which meant to them nothing more than the wild and heady thrill of victory over over-whelming odds; or the grim satisfaction of losing, of starting again with a laugh and a bitter joke and the uncomplaining tightening of their belts.

When it had been just a construction camp and division point, Esmeralda had been uproarious enough; but when a wandering prospector had panned flakes of yellow dust in the gravel that formed the lower slopes of towering Quentin Mountain, Esmeralda took a deep breath and roared the louder.

A genius by the name of Cale Coleman saw his opportunity and grasped it firmly. He brought in hydraulic machinery, and blasted down the gravel beds with eight-inch streams of fiercely driven water, manifolding the results obtained by the primitive methods of pan and cradle.

Cale Coleman was hard, arrogant, confident of his powers, not bothered much by false modesty and less by the other kind. Not bothered, either, by such mewlings as other men ascribed to qualms of conscience or fear of the possible consequence of their own acts.

"Get out of my way!" was Cale Coleman's motto and he never hesitated to apply it.

Neither Huck Brannon nor Lank Mason met Cale Coleman when, after seeing old Tom

Gaylord comfortably settled in the big new rail-road hospital, they went up to the Coleman mines in search of work. Cale was somewhere in the East buying more and improved machinery.

"Figger it's up to me to stick around until Tom is on his feet again," Huck told Mason. "It was mighty fine of Dunn to have him taken into the company hospital that way. I hear he gave orders Tom should have the best of everything and he's to stay until he's completely cured."

"Dunn took a shine to you, feller," Mason replied. "You'd oughta seed his eyes snap when that freight conductor told him how you stayed in the fire with yore shirt burnin' off yore back and your hair singein' to pull Tom loose. I got a notion that old general manager has a hefty likin' for skookum gents with guts and brains. He's that sort hisself."

The mine superintendent listened to their application and shrewdly appraised the potentialities of Huck's tall and vigorous form. He asked Lank Mason detailed technical questions and nodded with satisfaction.

"You know the ropes, all right," he commented. "I can use you over to the sluices as a foreman. Experienced men of your type ain't as handy as I'd like. Now as to you, young feller—"

He paused and his eye shifted to the far-flung battery of giant nozzles set on solid steel supports with ball joints that permitted a wide range of both horizontal and vertical play. From each nozzle hissed an eight-inch stream of muddy water driven with tremendous force and focused on the towering gravel-bank side of the mountain. Flanged wheels moved the platforms forward or back on narrow-gauge tracking. Lines of flexible pipe stretched down the mountainside to where giant rams provided the pressure. Huck noticed that two of the nozzles were not in operation.

The superintendent turned to the cowboy, probing him with his eyes. "You know anything 'bout hydraulic minin'?" he asked.

"Something about the engineering end, not very much about the practical side," Huck told him truthfully. "I never worked in the field."

The superintendent nodded. "Figgered as much. Well, you got the heft and you look like you have the brains. Think you could handle one of them big babies over yonder?"

"Show me how they work and I think I can," the cowpuncher replied.

"Okay, I'll give you a trial," the super decided. "It's a sorta ticklish job—not the kind for a lunk-head, like most of these muckers and rock busters are. Feller can do a awful lot of damage with one of them jets if he don't handle it just so —bust up machinery in a hurry and mebbe kill somebody.

"You got to keep yore eyes open ev'ry minute, not only to see how she's bringin' the gravel down, but to be shore she's p'inted right and there's nothin' in the way of the jet what hadn't oughta be. It's a job you can't sleep on, and one that needs quick thinkin' mighty often. That's why she pays top wages. Come 'long, and I'll have Casey, the foreman, put you onto handlin' the gun."

"Top wages is right," Huck said to Lank Mason later. "So far as the money end goes, this has shore got cow punchin' beat one helluva way. Don't know how I'll like it, but seeing as there aren't any spreads handy hereabouts, I reckon I can give it a shot until Old Tom is on his feet again."

It had never occurred to Huck Brannon until now that he might ever accept any job other than riding herd and punching cattle, even with the smattering of engineering that he'd studied. For him the life of the saddle, the open sky, the thud of pounding hoofs, the hot, sharp reek of branding irons against hide and hair came as natural and as welcome as breathing. It was in Brannon blood, deep-rooted. His father and his father's father and Brannons before them had lived their lives on the range.

However he quickly discovered that he did like the new work. There was a thrill to handling the thundering giant that pulsed and quivered beneath his hand, to seeing the reddish gravel, the packed earth and the embedded boulders dissolve like soft sugar under the impact of the crashing stream that bored into the mountainside with irresistible force. A mighty power was there at his fingertips, obedient to the slightest pressure of his hand, and capable, too, of appalling destruction.

Huck learned that there was an art to playing the stream correctly, adding to quickness of eye and hand keenness of perception and understanding of the terrain against which the stream was directed.

And the superintendent quickly learned that he had at No. Seven Nozzle a hand of no mean ability, a man who got results. Before two weeks had passed, he shifted Huck to No. One, at the far right end of the cutting. There unusual accuracy was called for in laying out the course up the mountainside—the course that would be followed by the other nozzlemen. And Huck got a raise.

"You're gettin' better'n foreman's pay now," Lank Mason said congratulating him.

The weeks passed swiftly—a month, six weeks, two months—and Old Tom was on his feet again, fully recovered.

"We'll discharge him the first of next week," the hospital superintendent told Huck. "Ordinarily we would have let him go last week or the week before, but Mr. Dunn's orders were very definite and nobody is anxious to violate the orders of Jaggers Dunn. It isn't apt to be healthy."

"You gonna quit when Gaylord gets out?"

Lank Mason asked Huck when he reported the news.

"Got a notion I'll hang on for a while," Huck told him. "Winter's right on top of us—gravel was froze so hard this morning I had to add pressure to bust the crust—and there isn't much doing in the cow business this time of year. Got a notion I'll hang on until Spring. It's not a bad job; and I sorta like this salty town. . . . Wasn't that fight in the Blue Whistler last night a lulu!"

Yes, the fight at the Blue Whistler had been a lulu. Huck, handy with fists himself, was something of an expert in the pugilistic art. But he hadn't gone to the fight because he liked to watch fights. He'd gone for the same reason these days he sought other diversions. To forget. To forget an amber-eyed, smiling, slender-limbed girl whose face haunted his dreams; the girl who, more than any other he'd ever seen, fitted into the pattern of his future. The girl he'd met before that future was sure enough for him to claim her.

Still he felt he had done the sensible thing. Getting away before he fell too much in love. He, a cowboy, worth less than the shirt on his back, dreaming about marriage, too soon. He had no business letting it happen. He would have preferred that his taking leave of the Bar X had been different. Not so abrupt. But since it had happened the way it had, he had to be content. It was a whole lot easier this way, in fact. No farewells, no painful explanations, no lingering doubts.

But now it was more than two months since he had last seen Sue Doyle; and her memory was just as strong and compelling as if it had been only the night before. The more he tried the harder it was to forget her. And each time she returned to his mind, she seemed prettier and more desirable.

The result was that he became moody, silent, preoccupied. Even at the saloon in that crowded, roaring roomful of revelers, he would suddenly forget what he was saying, forget the drink in his hand and go staring off into space. Several times Lank Mason had asked him what he was staring at—and had gotten only a grunt for an answer.

The only remedy he himself could find was work, work, and more work. He drove himself, working at the top of his strength all the time. He was pace-maker for the nozzlemen, and soon had outdistanced them in cutting his way up the mountainside. He strove hard and mightily to shut out the echo of a voice, the memory of a smile.

And for a while it seemed to succeed; but soon he found that the work had so built up his strength that it became increasingly difficult to achieve a fatigue that would let him sleep without dreaming. . . .

It was the morning after his conversation with

Lank Mason about Old Tom that Huck, busily pounding the frozen gravel with his "gun," heard a voice shouting peremptorily, its bellow carrying above the racket kicked up by the nozzle. A warning hiss sounded from the mechanic working at a minor repair.

"That's Coleman hisself, the Big Boss!"

Huck glanced to the right and saw a tall, broad man standing a yard or two beyond the play of the water jet. He was flashily dressed, had a square beefy face, long arms and huge hairy hands. His face was arrogant and ill-tempered, with a prominent straight nose, a straight mouth and straight black brows. Horizontal lines appeared to dominate the countenance that was in spite of its harshness, handsome in a sullen, rough-hewn style.

"Cut that jet farther to the right, you!" boomed the voice.

Huck obeyed, although his gray eyes narrowed slightly at Coleman's tone. He touched the nozzle control lightly, with perfect assurance, and the gleaming snout swung a trifle in its horizontal arc. The difference at the far end of the jet, where it beat against the gravel bank, was considerable.

Coleman watched the water smash the gravel, his face glowering and slightly flushed. He raised a big hand and knuckled his forehead savagely.

"He's got a pip of a hangover and wants to take it out on somebody," Huck guessed.

The mine-owner continued to glower at the cutting. The gravel was coming down swiftly, the jet hollowing out a beautifully straight furrow. The very skill of the performance seemed to anger Coleman further. He whirled, his eyes red and swollen with senseless anger.

"Blast the eyes off you!" he roared. "I said to cut that jet to the right, you thumping jackass!"

Huck Brannon's mouth suddenly clamped tight and his gray eyes turned smoky green. His right hand moved swiftly, surely, clamping hard on the control.

With a howl, Coleman leaped aside with cat-like agility, his face paper-white. The missing eight-inch stream grazed his coat. If it had struck him squarely, it would have killed him.

VIII

Written In Blood

Huck Brannon quietly stepped from the platform to the ground and stared coldly at the gasping Coleman.

"That far enough to the right?" he asked softly.

The scared white of Coleman's face abruptly burned fiery red. With a roar of fury he rushed at the cowpuncher, his fists flailing, curses spewing from his mouth.

Huck Brannon stepped lightly aside and struck, his left hand coming up from the level of his knee. His fist smacked against the big man's jaw with the spatting sound of a flat stone hitting the surface of a quiet pool. Coleman seemed to ripple through his whole six-foot length. His big body shot into the air and crashed down to the hard-frozen ground.

But it didn't stay. He came up like a cat off a hot stove, blood spurting from a long cut on his cheekbone, his face black with rage.

Huck instantly realized that he had a fight on his hands. Coleman was at least twenty-five pounds heavier, and he wasn't fat. He was perhaps an inch shorter than Huck, but his gorilla reach was longer. His fists working like pistons, he hurled himself at the cowpuncher, took a stunning right and left to the jaw, ducked his big head and kept coming.

Huck weaved, shifted, hammering out lefts and rights. Coleman grunted, spat blood and came on. He got through Huck's guard and spun him sideways with a mighty swing. Before Huck could recover, another blow caught him flush on the jaw.

Huck went down, head ringing, a taste of sulphur in his mouth. He rolled over just in time to escape the vicious kick Coleman launched at his body, streaked to his feet and knocked Coleman clean past the nozzle platform with a slashing left hook to the chin.

Again Coleman came to his feet, shaking his head, mumbling curses; and again he rushed, head down, thick arms flailing, more than willing to take a blow for every one he could give back.

Huck blocked his rush, clinched, and the two wrestled breast to breast, blowing bloody froth into each other's face from their cut lips, glaring with swollen eyes. Huck was dimly aware that they were surrounded by a yelling crowd; he heard Lank Mason's voice booming encouragement.

Coleman suddenly lifted him off his feet and hurled him down, hard. Huck landed on his left shoulder, skidded along the frozen ground. With a whoop of triumph Coleman rushed in to kick the life out of the prostrate cowboy.

Huck knew he could not get to his feet in time to block the rush. Coleman's heavy boots would smash him back before he got to his knees, and that would be the end. His brain worked at top speed, and with equal rapidity he whirled his sinewy legs toward the mine owner, kicking the right foot out with all his strength.

The booted sole caught Coleman on the knee.

At the same instant, Huck hooked his left foot behind Coleman's ankle and jerked.

There was a crackling sound, a yell of agony from Coleman and he fell to the ground, writhing and gasping. With another howl of pain he flopped over on his side and his hand streaked to his hip.

Lank Mason leaped forward, but Huck Brannon, bounding to his feet, was ahead of him. He kicked the gun from Coleman's hand even as Coleman pulled the trigger.

The crowd ducked and scattered at the roar of the shot and the screech of the slug that whipped a stinging red streak along the cowboy's bronzed cheek.

Huck picked up the big gun and thrust it in his belt.

"Been wantin' a gun quite a spell now," he said, panting and managing a bloody grin. "Thanks!"

"You get the hell off this property, you dirty killer!" Coleman bawled. "Get me to the hospital, some of you damned loafers, my leg's busted to hell!"

"Jest knocked out at the knee j'int, I figger," Lank Mason remarked as Coleman was carried away. "Well, get yore coat, feller, and let's mosey up and see if Tom Gaylord's ready to travel. Reckon we better be lookin' for a new stampin' ground now."

"He didn't fire you," Huck pointed out.

"Nope. I'm firin' myself," Lank said cheerfully. "I don't hanker to work for a horned toad what tries to kick a feller when he's on the ground, and goes for his gun when he's licked in a fair fight. C'mon, we'll stop at the office and get our pay. You'd better have them cuts on yore face washed out and plastered while we're at the hospital."

They found Old Tom smoking his pipe in comfort and staring speculatively out of the window toward where, raggedly cutting the western skyline, the saw-tooth peaks of the *Sangre de Cristo Range* loomed blue and misty in the distance. There was a gleam in his keen blue eyes as he listened to Lank's highly colored account of the fight.

"Which lets us out of a good job jest because the mines here happen to be owned by a skunk," concluded Lank. "Huck and me sorta cal'late on movin' on—mebbe inter Utah or over to Nevada—and we reckoned you might be int'rested in amblin' 'long with us, if you're feelin' pert 'nough by now."

"I'm feelin' pert, all right," Old Tom told them. "Woulda moseyed outa here last week if I'd made up my mind what my next move was. You fellers bein' set to trail yore rope sorta clears things up for me."

He paused, puffing at his pipe, turning something over in his mind. Finally he removed the stem from between his teeth, blew out a cloud of smoke and cleared his throat.

"You fellers," he began rather diffidently, "you fellers saved my life over to that wreck, and took mighty big chances on cashin' in yore own chips to do it. I ain't much on gabbin' and I can't say what I feel, but I jest want you to know I ain't fergettin' it."

He held up his hand as Huck and Lank began to disclaim any such heroics.

"Nev' mind all that—know what I'm talkin' 'bout and you fellers makin' light of what you did won't change it. What I got to say is I'm plumb gratful for what you did, and I aim to try and even it up by lettin' you in on somethin' big. Either of you ever hear tell of *La Mina del Padre?*"

Huck looked blank, but Lank Mason's eyes brightened with interest.

"The *Padre* Mine," he translated, "the lost *Padre* Mine? What minin' feller in the west ain't heerd tell of it?" He turned to Huck. "The story goes that there's five thousand bars of silver, mebbe more, hid in that mine—silver that Don Fernando de Castro, the Spaniard, and old Padre Diego Escalante made the Injuns mine for them. Story says Don Fernando was so 'fernal mean to the Injuns that the tribes got t'gether and wiped him and his men out, includin' the padre, who'd allus tried to be their friend. But 'fore they was attacked they managed to hide the silver in the mine and hide the mine, too. That's the yarn you hear down in the Southwest, but I figger it's jest a yarn, like lots of others."

Old Tom slowly shook his head.

"It ain't a yarn," he said, "it's the God's truth."

"What makes you think so, oldtimer?"

" 'Cause I got the map old Padre Diego drew 'fore he died—the map what shows where the lost mine's at."

Lank Mason guffawed, his belly bobbing up and down like a seal beside an iceberg. "Yeah, ev'body's got a map," he said. "Lots of 'em for sale down in the Southwest. I knowed a feller what raised a family of kids and sent 'em through school sellin' maps of lost mines and hid gold and such."

Tom Gaylord said nothing. But he drew from his pocket a huge cowhide wallet, opened it, and took out a package wrapped in oiled silk. He unwrapped the silk and spread out on his knee an irregular fragment of linen, yellowed and old. Upon it, faded rusty words were dimly visible.

"Ever see a map like *this* one?" he asked quietly.

Lank picked up the fragment of linen, a wondering expression on his face. He examined the irregular tracing, translated the Spanish words with muttering lips. Huck Brannon, also eyeing the peculiar document, saw Lank's begin to blaze with excitement.

Lank stabbed at the tracing with a great hairy sausage of a finger, scratched a line lightly with a blunt nail.

"Blood!" he muttered. "Writ in blood, shore as hell! Why this damn thing must be nigh onto a hundred years old!"

He wet his lips, staring harder at the lines and markings. "Hell, I know this country!" he exclaimed. "See—there's the twin Spanish Peaks marked plain, and the Apishapa River, and Carson's Peak, and Dominguez Crik in its narrer canyon! Gaylord, where did you get this thing?"

Old Tom chuckled, glancing shrewdly at the miner's flushed face.

"Get's you, eh? It got me, too, and I don't know the section like you do—jest the gen'ral lay of the land. I got that map from an old Mexican down El Paso way. It was handed down to him by his grandpappy who claimed it was give to him by the old padre who drew it on the tail of his shirt with his blood after the Injuns had ambushed Don Fernando and his men while they was tryin' to make it back to Mexico.

"The padre told the greaser, who was jest a boy then, to take the map and the wordin' on it to Mexico and turn it over to the Officers of the King of Spain. But 'fore the boy got there, the rev'lution had took place and there weren't no king's officers in Mexico any more. His mother told him the rag was sacred 'cause it had the padre's blood on it and the family should keep it so it'd bring 'em good luck.

"The old feller I got it from said it hadn't never brought 'em anythin' but bad luck, so far as he could make out—I'd jest saved him from starvin' with a broken leg in the Cuevas salt desert and he was sorta grateful to me. 'Sides, he'd got the notion inter his haid that the rag with the blood on it might be to blame for his trouble. I'd run onter it when I went through his clothes while he was still unconscious, tryin' to find out who he might be in case he cashed in, and when I asked him 'bout it, he told me the story. He was plumb willin' to let me have the rag for a handful of pesos."

Huck Brannon was of a practical turn of mind.

"Why didn't he, or his father or grandfather, go after the silver?" he asked.

"I gather they figgered there was a curse on it," replied Gaylord. "I cal'late there was a lot more to the yarn than what my greaser remembered. Details sorta get lost with ignorant folks like that after a gen'ration or two. He couldn't even read the words wrote on the rag and I don't figger he knowed there was sich a place as Colorado.

"If I hadn't happened to know somethin' 'bout this section, I'd never been able to figger it out from the map. All he could say was that his grand-pappy brought it from the mountains of the north. That nacherly meant northern New Mexico or Colorado—that's 'bout as far north as the Spaniards ever got lookin' for gold and silver —and I figgered the rest. What you say, fellers, willin' to give it a whirl with me?"

"Count me in," Lank replied instantly. "I really b'lieve you got somethin' here. What you think, Brannon?"

Huck laughed. "I'm afraid I haven't much faith in the yarn," he admitted, "but we haven't anything particularly pressing on hand just now, and from what you say, the section is less than fifty miles off. So why not?"

Lank arose with alacrity. "We'll get an outfit t'gether pronto," he said. "Picks, shovels, blastin' powder, grub. I'll 'tend to them. Huck, see if you can pick up a coupla burros—I seed some over to the Mexican quarter t'other day. Bring 'long that gun you took off Coleman; I think I'll try and pick up a shotgun—grouse and sich sorta busts up the monotony of bacon and beans."

The following morning Cale Coleman, lying in an upper story bed beside the window, saw them pass the hospital, loaded burros wagging long ears with simulated docility, the tall figure of Huck Brannon striding in front.

The mine owner craned his neck, cursed viciously as a twinge shot through his leg, and glared murder after the passing forms. A moment later, however, a speculative gleam replaced the angry light in his eyes. He summoned an orderly and gave him profane instructions. A little later his drift foreman, Jeff Eades, clumped into the room.

Eades was big, almost as big as his boss, with a hard face, a tight mouth and uncertain eyes. He listened in silence to what Coleman had to say, nodding his head from time to time.

"Okay," he said when Coleman had finished. "I'll put Esteban on the trail. We'll find out, and then we'll even things up."

Coleman sank back on his pillow after his foreman had departed, in his eyes a look of subtle satisfaction.

IX

Stumped

Kansas City was only a three-week-old memory to Huck Brannon in Esmeralda, on the day that Sue Doyle stepped off the train at the big wood-shed station.

She strode purposefully down the street. She had been to Kansas City before and knew her way around. Her immediate destination was Ma Hennessey's rooming house, where the boys had spent the night, before returning to the Bar X.

The house, a dingy, gray-boarded two-story affair she remembered, was located at the other end of the street. As she walked along, her father's parting words buzzed through her brain.

"Yuh're makin' a big mistake chasin' after him, Sue," he had said. "Even if he is the son of my old friend."

But she had been adamant.

There was one question Sue was glad her father hadn't asked her, for she didn't know the answer herself. And that question was what she would do if she did find Huck? She avoided it like the plague, but it returned continually to torment her. The iron clank of the wheels on the train that bore her here had flung the question at her, and the crunch of her boot in the dirt echoed it.

She still felt the shock of his lips meeting hers, of his arms suddenly thrown around her, of the queer, half-surprised light in his eye, of the eager look on the face that stared after her. At least, she had thought it was eager then. Now in the face of Huck's desertion, she wondered. At one moment, she was sure of it. *Sure.* Then a doubt would spring up in her mind. Over and over, endlessly. Certainty, doubt, then certainty again.

Again she asked herself why that sudden kiss had happened this time. She had seen Huck off on previous trips, many times, and the good-bye had been casual, friendly. But this time, without warning, emotion had swept over her like a stampeding herd, leaving her giddy and faint. Why? She could not say. All she knew was that when she saw Huck Brannon on the point of leaving, she hadn't wanted him to go.

She had told her father that she wasn't sure when he asked her if she had gone soft on that "young hellion." But now she knew. Not only *soft,* but soft enough to go chasing after him, determined to find him if it meant staying on his trail for months.

It was true she had little to go on, so far as his feelings were concerned—only that look on his face which she was certain she had seen when she kissed him. That and the many hours they had spent together. Certain things which seemed inexplicable then, but on which her new emotions had shed new light. Once he had gazed at her with an odd, questioning look in his eye, then quickly turned when he saw she was watching him. And told her that he meant to settle down with a family as soon as he had the money to buy a spread and stock it with cattle.

She had brought up the question of his being so footloose. Then she had pointed out that to raise a family he first needed a wife. She remembered his reply:

"Why, sure, Sue, that's what I've been thinking.

As a matter of fact, I reckon I've got one already picked out."

A sharp pang had cut through her heart like a knife. But now she recalled it half hopefully—almost sure he had meant her. And she blamed herself for having been so blind then. Because he'd never spoken to her that way again.

The square sign, lettered in black and nailed beside the door read, *Rooming House.* Underneath these two words, in smaller characters: *M. Hennessey, Prop.*

She had heard vague reports of Ma Hennessey, and had composed a picture of her out of scraps of talk on the boys' returns from Kansas City. Why the boys continued to frequent this particular rooming house, she could never understand, for Ma Hennessey was reputed to have a roaring, slashing tongue and the disposition of a catamount. But year after year the Bar X kept going back.

She had also heard that Ma Hennessey was a giantess afraid of no man—and was physically capable of bouncing out any puncher for whatever reason. Indeed, one of the boys swore he had seen her pick up a puncher in her two big hands and heave him through the nearest window as casually as she would bite into an apple.

In spite of all these warnings, Sue was hardly prepared for the figure that answered her knock.

Ma Hennessey stood about six feet four, with

a frame that filled the doorway. Hulking arms, like an ape's, hung down her sides. And attached to their ends were two huge paws with fingers of iron.

But what struck Sue most was Ma Hennessey's face. Separated from the body, it would have been difficult to decide whether the face was a man's or woman's. In fact, it looked neither. It possessed a cold, sexless hardness that was repellently fascinating.

"Well—what do you want?" Like her face, Ma Hennessey's voice was hard and expression-less.

"I wonder if you can help me?" asked Sue.

"Looking for a room?"

"No—I was looking for—"

"This is a rooming house, miss. If you ain't looking for a room, you better go somewhere else." Ma Hennessey started to close the door in Sue's face.

"No—wait, please." There was a note of appeal in her voice.

For a moment Ma hesitated, then she snapped: "What do you want?"

"Huck Brannon, of the Bar X Ranch, Stevens Gulch, Texas, stopped here about three weeks ago with the rest of the boys. Do you know what happened to him? He hasn't returned to the ranch."

"That drunken rapscallion—"

"He is not! I won't let you talk like that about him," Sue said very firmly.

Ma Hennessey gazed at Sue queerly for a moment and a glint came to her eye. She seemed to unbend a little.

"Keep your shirt on, lady. Are you his sister?"

She could feel her face heat. "No," she said. "He rides for my father."

"Oh! So you're Sue Doyle."

"How do you know my name?"

"Your drunken cowboy spent the whole livelong night singing and shouting your name at the top of his lungs."

Sue's heart leaped. A sudden fever ran through her veins.

"He isn't my cowboy," she protested helplessly.

"So the rancher's daughter falls in love with her old man's rider," Ma mocked, "and comes running after him when he don't come runnin' home to the ranch."

Anger coursed through Sue's brain and she could hardly keep back her furious retort. Ma might know where Huck had gone, and if she did, Sue wanted to learn it. And something told her she'd find out nothing if she made Ma angry.

"It doesn't matter why I came looking for Mr. Brannon," she said. "All I asked is what you know about what happened to him."

"Nothing!" snapped Ma Hennessey. "Nothing happened to your cowboy. He came in roaring drunk and singing and I told him to shut up or I'd throw him out. So he shut up and went to sleep. The other boys left early, but your *Mr. Brannon* slept nearly to noon and then cleared out. I would have charged him for another day if he stayed one minute later."

"But where did he go?"

"How do I know?" snapped the woman. "I ain't his Ma. The last I seen of him, he was cutting across to them railroad yards."

"Thank you, Mrs. Hennessey. Thank you very much. You've been very kind," Sue lied.

Ma Hennessey glared at Sue, shouted an angry, "Bah" at her and slammed the door. But Sue was beyond caring about Ma's rugged manners.

All she could think of was that Huck Brannon had sung and shouted her name. She was no longer in doubt. But she was certain now that something had happened to Huck.

Suddenly her heart contracted. Suppose he was hurt—hurt badly and needed her care? She brushed the thought from her mind, as she turned rapidly back to the railroad station.

She was oblivious of the hot sun beating down on her, of the men flirting with her from street-sides—of everything—until she reached the station shed.

The ticket agent, although interested and sympathetic, was unable to give Sue any helpful information—except that he remembered selling a batch of tickets for Stevens Gulch to a flock of cowboys some weeks back. He was certain no one answering the description of Huck Brannon bought a ticket later that same day for Stevens Gulch. As a matter of fact, he assured Sue, no one had bought any tickets for the Gulch since that one morning.

Sue groaned inwardly. "You're sure you don't remember him?" she asked for the tenth time.

"I'm sartain, ma'am," the agent replied kindly. It was evident that the young lady was deeply distressed. "Say, why don't you try the yard-master. Mebbe he seen him."

Sue, following his directions, walked down the railroad yard, threaded her way past a line of empties, crossed ties and tracks and finally located the yardmaster at a caboose. He was directing the loading of railroad ties and piles for construction work somewhere on the line. He turned when one of his men pointed to Sue.

He was a squat, bulky, bald-headed man and stood mopping his sweat-beaded forehead with a large gray kerchief as Sue repeated her questions. When she began describing Huck, he gave a start, brought his hand down from his head and peered hard at her.

"If that's the man I think it is," he snapped, "*we're* lookin' for him, too."

Sue's heart leaped. "You recognize that description?"

"Shore," the yardmaster snorted. "That's the hellion who put Fred Rowles in the hospital for two weeks with a busted head. We been hankerin' to lay our hands on that hobo."

"What do you mean?" Sue cried.

The yardmaster told Sue about the fracas in the railroad yards when two hobos, trying to get a free ride, were discovered by Fred Rowles who tried to throw them off the train and was badly beaten up by one of them.

"That sounds like Huck."

"Lucky for him," the yardmaster concluded, "that Rowles came outa this alive, or there would've been a murder charge on this hombre's head."

"But what happened to him? Did you catch him?"

"No, dashblame it," the man growled. "Him an' the other feller gave us the slip."

"Where could they have gone?"

"I wish you could tell me, ma'am," he said grimly. "The boys would kinda like to get their hands on both of them. But they run out on us. Mebbe they hopped the train goin' east—and mebbe they hopped the train headed west. Think most likely it was east—that freight left quicker than the westbound."

"Oh."

Sue thanked him and headed back to the station. The first joy at finding some trace of Huck had already gone, and disappointment was taking its place. There was no doubt in her mind that it *was* Huck who had been involved in the fighting.

The dispatch and ease with which he had handled the railroad detective fitted the Huck who had given a hiding to a town bully who had boldly accosted her on the street in Stevens Gulch several months before.

And the important thing was that Huck was all right—even if she hadn't found him.

According to the yardman, he was headed east. Probably, Sue thought, because he feared he had murdered the "bull" and was running away. Running away didn't sound like Huck. But she was forced to admit that it provided the first good reason she had found for Huck's failure to return to the Bar X.

As Sue reconstructed it, Huck, out of funds and too proud to wire for money, had decided to hop a freight and ride back to Stevens Gulch —she knew how any cowboy detests walking. Apparently he had picked up a companion and together they tried to find an open car, when they were surprised by the railroad "bull." Huck had beaten the man in a fist fight; but then another "bull" came along and before Huck had time to discover how badly hurt the first man was, he had to flee. Then, fearing he had killed the man, and knowing the obvious consequences, he had impulsively decided to get away.

Sue Doyle accepted this gratefully, for it left her her pride. Huck hadn't deserted her. Her kiss hadn't driven him away. The telegram she sent her father when she got to the station was brief and business-like:

DEAR DAD: ON HIS TRAIL. TAKING THE TRAIN EAST. LOVE. SUE.

X

The Broken Trail

It was wild and lonely there in the shadow of the towering Twin Peaks, with the rugged battlements of the *Sangre de Cristo* Range marching majestically into the northwest. It was a land of bare black rock and rushing white water, where the scream of the eagle sounded by day and the lonely shriek of the stalking panther by night.

Streams foamed at the bottom of deep canyons and barrancas. The wind was bitter on the heights and snow lay in the crotches of the beeches and on the shaded sides of rocks.

The ground was hard-frozen and the rustle of dead leaves and the creak of the mesquite thorns accentuated the harshness of the winter landscape.

And yet it had not been a too-arduous trek for Huck and his companions. They followed the water-level route, by way of the river at first, to the terrain encompassed by the old priest's map; then turned sharply to thread the winding course of Dominguez Creek.

Lank Mason exclaimed from time to time as familiar landmarks compared accurately to those pricked out in blood on the scrap of yellowed linen.

"That old feller had oughta been a surveyor," he declared. "Takin' the Peaks and Carson for his anchor stones, he lined the trail perfect. Right ahaid now is Dominguez Creek Canyon or I'm a packrat!"

Lank was right. They came out on a mesa and, several miles distant, was the dark mouth of the gorge with the turbulent stream tumbling from it.

"Don't hardly ever anybody come inta this section," observed Lank. "Badlands and hole-in-the-wall country from here on. Mighty nigh impossible to get out any way 'cept the way we come in. Nothin' here, so far as anybody knows, and one glim at them hills and rocks to the west and nawth is 'nough to head prospectors or anybody else back the way they come. Reckon that's the reason nobody ain't ever tumbled onto what we're lookin' for."

"That is, if we're really looking for *something*," Brannon said, with a grin.

"You wait and see," Lank declared stubbornly. "I'm plumb sartain the oldtimer here has got somethin'."

Huck grinned again, and said no more. And it was his keen eyes that discovered the first tangible proof of the authenticity of map and legend.

They were approaching the mouth of the canyon, threading their way with difficulty through the dense growth that choked the banks of the stream, when Huck's attention was caught by a gleam of white.

At first he thought it was only a rain-washed stone, but a second look told him what it really was—a skull, bleached and dried but still intact in outline despite the weathering of more than half a century.

He picked it up, with the others crowding close to stare at the dread symbol of man's mortality. Huck's eyes narrowed as he examined the hollow bone.

"Not an Indian's," he said bluntly.

With added interest he began poking about among the growth. Soon they found other skulls, and other fragments of skeletons. Some of the skulls were plainly Indian, but the majority, Huck was convinced, were of white men.

With an exclamation, Lank Mason suddenly plucked something from beside the gnarled trunk of a giant mesquite. He held it up, a length of rusty steel, worn thin and narrow by the ravages of the elements. It was a section of a rusty sword.

"Busted off 'bout half way up," said the miner.

"And here's somethin' what looks like a old tin pot half buried in this crack," Old Tom called.

"What's left of a steel helmet," Huck told him, his gray eyes glowing with excitement. "Gents, it seems as if there'd been a pretty hefty scrap here a long time back."

"The ruckus when the Injuns wiped out the Spaniards," Old Tom insisted.

"Looks like it, all right," the cowpuncher admitted. "And it begins to look like there's something to this yarn of yours, after all."

"I told you so!" Lank Mason crowed. But it was Lank who was due to voice pessimism before a second sun had set.

Straight to the mouth of the canyon the faded line on the map pointed, and then to its further end. So they made their way there, and paused to stare at the foaming rush of water where Dominguez Creek leaped over the end wall of the box canyon, the crest of which was nearly a hundred feet above the gorge floor.

"This don't look so good," growled Lank. "Map p'ints right up to here, but there ain't no mine here, and no place for one to be."

"The stuff's prob'ly buried some place 'round here, that's what I been thinkin' all the time," Old Tom remarked cheerfully.

It wasn't. By evening of the following day, all three were firmly convinced of that. They had covered every foot of the ground in the canyon, and found nothing to substantiate even remotely Gaylord's belief. The crumbling remains of some rickety cabins along the west wall of the canyon were the only indication that anybody had ever entered the gorge.

"And the chances are they was used by trappers and hunters back in the days when skins was wuth more than they are now," Lank grumbled as he gloomily prepared supper.

But Huck, formerly the most skeptical member of the trio, stubbornly refused to be discouraged.

"I'm getting more and more convinced that there really is something here," he declared. "The fact that we don't find it right off the bat doesn't prove the thing just a wild yarn. Anything of real value *would* be carefully hidden. As Lank says, there used to be lots of hunters and trappers in these hills—lots more than there are now—and whoever had anything to hide would take that into account and not lay it on top of a rock or out in the sun where anybody happening along would stumble onto it."

"We've follered the map to right where it shows," Lank pointed out. "Here at the head of the canyon is where the line peters out."

"Tom, let's see that map again," Huck said.

Old Tom brought forth the yellowed linen and

Huck studied it earnestly, the concentration furrow deepening between his black brows. At length he exclaimed sharply.

"I see it now," he declared. "Part of this map is gone. We haven't got the whole thing."

Their heads bent eagerly forward to scan the dingy linen.

"What you mean—how you figger?" asked Old Tom.

Huck pointed to the diagonal edge of the cloth.

"See," he said, "all the rest of the edges show they were torn loose from a bigger piece. This edge here wasn't torn. See how regular it is, and unraveled. Once this thing was just about square. This slantwise edge was cut clean with a knife."

"And s'posin' it was—what does that mean?" asked Lank. "You can see plain we got all the map tracin' here—the line of the trail begins and ends before it gets to the edges."

"Yes," replied Huck, "but what we haven't got, or I'm mistaken, is the part on which the old padre wrote instructions how to locate the stuff after you get to the head of the canyon. For some reason or other, that's been cut away."

"And s'posin' that's so, what we gonna do 'bout it?"

"For one thing, tomorrow, we're going up on top of these canyon walls and see if we can run onto anything interesting. I've got a hunch the key to this thing is up there somewhere. Anyway, I figure it's worth trying."

Nobody objected and they ate supper in a more cheerful frame of mind.

And while the partners put away their chuck, washing it down with cups of steaming coffee, beady black eyes watched their every move from the canyon wall and thin lips moved back from yellowed teeth in a humorless grin. . . .

"I reckon we'll hafta troop clean back to the mouth of this damn hole-in-the-wall 'fore we can get up topside the walls," Lank complained the following morning.

"Unless we can find some way up the sides," Huck agreed.

They found such a way, and at no great distance below their camp. It was a deep ravine, or dry watercourse rather, scored in the canyon wall. Not an easy ascent, and Lank was puffing hard when he finally crawled over the ragged lip. Huck stared about with interest, his steady eyes narrowed and intent.

The ravine ended in a comparatively narrow depression, very deep for its width, its sloping sides choked by growth. They could see it winding away to the north, diagonaling toward the course of Dominguez Creek.

"Must have been a lot of water coming down here one time," Huck observed. "Why, I wonder —and why doesn't it come this way now?"

"Mebbe the crick run this way onct," suggested Gaylord.

"The creek is flowing through what is actually slightly higher ground," Huck pointed out. "Water doesn't run uphill. That is, unless somebody helps it," he added, his dark brows drawing closer together.

Lank looked bewildered, but Old Tom cocked a speculative eye at the cowboy. "You found out somethin'?" he asked.

"Wait," Huck said.

They followed the depression, Huck leading the way. Lank and Old Tom scrutinized the growth-covered sides for some signs of shaft or tunnel or significant mound; but Huck's attention was centered on the course of the peculiar gully. He appeared impatient of delay and forged ahead of his companions.

XI

La Mina del Padre?

The grade rose sharply as they progressed northward, and the sound of the waters of Dominguez Creek grew steadily louder. Soon the bed of the depression was very nearly on a level with that of the creek.

101

The bed itself interested Huck. It was mostly naked rock, shelving somewhat, its surface worn smooth by the action of water, although now not even a trickle could be detected. Tufts of grass sprouted from the cracks, and here and there a clump of brush strove for a footing in a patch of shallow soil.

Once, however, rooted in a deep and wide cleft, a sturdy blue spruce shot up its silver and pale blue cone to whisper softly in the wind.

The cowpuncher halted and regarded the tree with quickened interest. "How old you figger this feller to be?"

"Forty-fifty years, mebbe more; why?" replied Mason.

"Pine trees don't grow in the water," Huck answered.

"Not so's I ever noticed," admitted Lank.

"Which means that there hasn't been any water in this gully for a mighty long time."

"Uh-huh."

"And the signs show that there was a lot here at one time. What's the answer?"

"The answer, I'd say," replied Lank, "is that onct 'pon a time, years ago, Dominguez Crick ran down here 'stead of up where it is."

"Exactly," Huck replied, adding ironically: "And then she turned 'round and ran up hill for a change. C'mon, let's go."

A few minutes later he turned abruptly and

began climbing the steep bank. He topped it and less than fifty yards distant, he could see the rushing waters of Dominguez Creek. A couple of hundred yards upstream, the creek bank and the dry wash joined to form a V; the bed of the dry wash was considerably higher than that of the creek.

Huck pointed this out to the others and then silently indicated the precise banks of the stream downward from the point of contact to the lip of the falls, more than half a mile distant.

"From here to the falls, the creek follows a course never intended by nature," he said quietly. "They dug a channel, strengthening the sides with boulders and broken stone, and turned the creek into it. Below here the old creek bed is at a lower level than the new, but from here up it's higher."

"After they had the new channel constructed, it was simple to blow the bank at this point and turn the water into it, sending it over the end canyon wall instead of over the side wall nearly a mile farther down by way of the course the stream originally followed."

"But why did they do that?" Lank demanded.

"That's what we're going to find out," Huck told him quietly. "They didn't do it for fun, that's sure. We're going to gamble a few charges of blasting powder to get the answer. Let's get back to camp for tools and cartridges."

"You figger they hid the stuff in the crick?" Old Tom panted, wild with excitement, as they hurried back down the wash.

Huck shook his head. "No, I figure they hid the mouth of the mine with the creek," he replied. "Where does the trail as mapped out by the old padre end? Right at the head of the canyon. And what's at the head of the canyon? The waterfall made by the creek following the built channel. What we're looking for is back of that falls, and I'm willing to bet my last peso on it."

"And I wouldn't risk a plugged dime bettin' 'gainst you!" boomed Lank Mason. "C'mon, you mud turtles. Get a move on!"

They scrambled down the wash to the canyon floor and hurried toward the camp, with Huck in the lead.

Suddenly the cowboy's hand streaked to the butt of the big gun he had kicked from Cale Coleman's hand. But before he could line sights on the flickering shadow fleeing the site of the camp, it had dived into the growth and vanished.

Huck raced to the straggle of chapparal, weaving and ducking to provide as difficult a target as possible. But there was no need of caution. Nothing moved in the growth and his sharp eyes could find no evidence of recently broken brush.

"Wolverine, the chances are," said Lank. "Damn

pests are allus rootin' 'round camps and tearin' things up."

Huck was examining the ground around the camp, which on the side next the chaparral was moist because of the overflow of a small spring. He pointed to a print in the partially frozen mud.

"Wolverines don't wear moccasins," he observed.

Lank and Old Tom examined the print.

"Injun," Lank decided. "A snoopin' buck from a mine camp or somewhere. Wonder he didn't steal ev'thin' that was loose. Reckon he woulda if he'd had time."

Huck indicated the seepage of water into the print. It was delicately filmed with ice.

"He was here quite a spell back, from the looks of that," he told the others. "See if anything is missing."

Nothing was, but one of the packs showed slight but unmistakable signs of meticulous search.

" 'Pears he *was* lookin' for somethin'," said Gaylord. "Now what in blazes—"

"Appears somebody is taking an interest in what we're doing," Huck supplemented a trifle grimly. "I've a notion it won't hurt to keep our eyes peeled from now on. Well, let's get those tools together and do this job 'fore dark."

Huck's knowledge of engineering, slight though it was, proved invaluable when com-

bined with native shrewdness and his cattleman's instinct for topographical features. Lank, of
course, knew all there was to know about plant-
ing powder charges.

From a safe distance they saw huge stones and
masses of earth burst through the fluff of smoke
as the echoes rolled backward and forward
between the mountain walls. For an instant the
waters of the creek seemed to poise, hesitate;
then, with a thunder that drowned the echoes of
the explosion, they went rushing and foaming
down the dry wash which had been their course
for untold ages before man appeared on the
scene.

The falls thinned as if by magic, dwindled to a
trickle that went crawling down the black and
glistening wall of rock and soon ceased altogether.
Along the bed was left only dark pools that
marked scoured-out places in the floor of the
man-made channel.

Huck and his friends, however, gave scant
attention to the drained channel. They were hurrying toward the distant mouth of the canyon, their
path down the dry wash of course being blocked
by the rush of the water which now used it as a
way to the canyon floor. The end wall overhung
and made descent there impossible.

The winter sun was lying low in the west and
pouring a flood of reddish light into the gloomy
canyon when they reached the site of their

camp. They burst through the final fringe of growth and stood staring.

Where there had been a down-rush of foam-flecked water was now only glistening rock, filming with ice which reflected the reddish light until the whole wall seemed to flow with sluggish blood. At the base of the wall was a black opening from which trickled a steady stream of water.

The opening was regular in outline, arched at the top, sufficiently wide and high for the passage of several mules abreast.

"There she is," Huck Brannon said quietly. "There's *La Mina del Padre!*"

Old Tom's eyes were bright and shining. Lank breathed heavily.

"The Lost Padre Mine," he repeated. "Well, gents, it looks like all we got to do is walk in and collect."

If any of them had had any inkling of the suffering, destruction and death that they would collect in these black depths beyond the gloomy portal framed in bloody light, possibly not one of them would have taken another step in its direction.

But perhaps some dim premonition of what was to come did cause them to hesitate upon the threshold. Even Huck Brannon, although he would have been unable to name his reason, was reluctant to lead the way into that frowning opening in the blood-streaked cliff.

Old Tom gave voice to the general uneasiness.

"It's late," he said, "and we've had a mighty hard day. S'pose we get us a mess o' chuck and eat. Then it'll be time for a little shuteye. We'll need to fix up somethin' to take 'long with us, incidentally—no tellin' how long we may hafta prowl 'round in that diggin' 'fore we hit onto what we're lookin' for. What say, fellers?"

They nodded agreement; and so it was the morning sun, flooding the canyon with brilliance and turning the withered leaves into flakes of dead gold, that saw them approach the dark gap in the cliff face. There was a frosty bite to the air and the film of ice glittered cheerfully. The little stream trickling from the mouth of the old mine chuckled to itself as it hurried along the former channel to join Dominguez Creek farther down the canyon.

They had brought Davey lamps and Huck carefully adjusted the flames inside their covering of protective gauze. And before they had advanced a hundred yards along the ancient tunnel, he congratulated himself on his choice of safety lamps. For Lank Mason was wrinkling his nose like a rabbit and his sniffs echoed loudly against the side walls.

"Gas o' some kind," he declared. "I can smell it strong. Don't do any lightin' up of smokes, gents, till we're plumb shore what it is. Might be explosive."

Huck nodded and pointed to the lamps. The protective gauze showed slightly pinkish, a sure sign of inflammable gas in the air.

"Funny," mused the cowboy. "What's that sort of gas doing in a silver mine?"

"Never can tell," replied Lank. "Why, over to some of the diggin's 'round Trinidad, you're allus sniffin' some bad smellin' stuff."

XII

Don Fernando's Legacy

Soon side galleries made their appearance, branching off from the main artery at various angles. At the first of these Huck hesitated, then decided to follow the original tunnel to the end and leave investigation of its branching burrows until later.

For nearly a mile the gallery pierced the mountain's heart, following a comparatively straight line. Then, without warning, it ended in a wide and high chamber which the cowboy decided was a natural formation.

"Here's where they stored the stuff, chances are," Lank exclaimed, peering into the gloom beyond the small circle of radiance cast by the lamps.

"There's somethin' over there to the left," said Gaylord. "Let's see what it is."

They turned in that direction, and a moment later Lank halted, to stand with outthrust head, staring at what the glow of the lamps revealed. Involuntarily he retreated a step from his gruesome find. Old Tom shuffled nervously. Huck Brannon, stepping ahead of Lank, felt the hairs of his scalp prickle. He advanced closer, the lamp held high.

Row on row they lay, some in distorted attitudes, bony knees drawn up to touch grinning jaws. Some were mere yellowish skeletons held together by some vestiges of sinew. In others a parchment-like covering of skin was drawn tightly over protruding ribs and eyeless skulls. On the faces of these last, withered, inhuman though they were, it seemed to Huck that there was indelibly stamped the horror and terror and unutterable anguish that preceded death.

Fastened to each shrunken ankle was an iron band from which a heavy chain led to a ring set in the stone wall.

"Good God?" breathed Old Tom. "What are them things?"

Huck Brannon stared at the pitiful remains that were a monument to man's cruelty and greed. His eyes were hard and cold as he replied:

"The Indian slaves who worked the mine. Left here to starve and die of thirst."

"But why?" Gaylord asked.

A thought suddenly struck Huck, a disquieting thought.

"Maybe they knew something the Spaniards didn't want told. Recollect how the old pirates used to kill the men who buried their treasure? 'Dead men tell no tales!' Maybe that's the answer. Well, let's see what else is in this graveyard."

They found evidence that the chamber had been used to house the slaves. There were crude stone tables, rusted tools, the remains of cooking utensils. Blackened places showed where fires had been kindled.

That was all. Circling around, they reached the end wall and found the source of the little stream which trickled down the main tunnel.

Water streaked the black and shining surface of the wall, seeping in minute drops from the stone, the drops gathering at the base to form the stream.

Huck eyed the wall with a dubious eye.

"Must be a lot of water back of there," he told his companions. "The weight of it is driving it through the rock, and the chances are the rock is mighty thick."

"The gas is mighty thick here, too," grumbled Lank. "S'pose we go take a look at some of them galleries. That's likely where the stuff is, or the veins it was worked. All we need is to find them veins."

They didn't find them, although there was plenty of evidence that they had once existed. What they did find were other specimens of the glistening black stone at the end wall of the chamber of death.

Those veins of dark stone interested Huck; but they brought only disgust and depression to his companions. Finally Lank Mason sat down with a bitter curse. They had been prowling the galleries for hours and had covered every foot of the mine.

"Worked out!" he growled. "Worked out, shore as shootin'! No wonder the Spaniards shoved off. They'd cleaned up. They either sent all the stuff to Mexico ahaid of 'em or were takin' it with 'em when the Injuns jumped 'em. Then of course the Injuns carried it off with *them*—mebbe hid it somewhere."

"But in that case, why'd the old priest go to the trouble to draw a map that'd tell folks how to get to this place?" Gaylord asked.

"Mebbe he jest wanted to show folks what a rat the feller that bossed the outfit was," Lank grunted. "Chances are, though, he thought there was still lots of silver here. A padre wouldn't know much 'bout minin'."

Old Tom nodded. "Reckon yore right," he admitted dully. "Well, gents, looks like we'll hafta go back to diggin' and ropin' for a livin'. That the way you figger it, Huck?"

Huck Brannon stood up, stretching his long arms. He grinned down at his partners.

"Nope," he said, "I don't. Unless I'm making a great big mistake, and I don't believe I am, *I* figure we got something here worth a lot more than the silver mine ever was!"

Tom Gaylord and Lank stared at Huck as if he had gone insane.

"I knowed he'd hadn't oughta et them last four jerky sandwiches!" Lank wailed. "Or mebbe it was the coffee!"

"What in blazes you talkin' 'bout, son?" demanded Old Tom.

Huck grinned at them. He took a pick and walked briskly to the glistening end-wall of the gallery.

"I suspected it there in the big room," he said, "and after looking over the rest of these tunnels, I'm certain of it."

As he spoke he struck sharply with the pick and brought down a shower of fragments from the wall. He rubbed one against the palm of his hand, leaving a black smudge on the flesh.

Old Lank stared at the dark streak, snatched the fragment from Huck's hand and turned it over in his blunt fingers.

"Good gosh!" he exclaimed incredulously. "Darned if I don't b'lieve it is—"

He hesitated, and Huck finished the sentence for him: "Yes, it's coal."

"Coal in a silver mine!" Old Tom scoffed. "Whoever heerd tell of sich foolishment!"

"It's not foolishness," Huck replied. "This is a semi-bituminous coal, verging on anthracite. One of the means anthracite is produced is by the intrusion of molten igneous rocks upon the coal beds. The gangue of silver is most always quartz, an igneous rock."

"Yeah, you most allus find silver mixed up in quartz," agreed Lank.

"This silver mine was a sorta freak deposit of native silver. The veins didn't go deep like in the Comstock and such deposits. It was easy to mine, but soon played out. Looks like old Don Fernando cleaned up 'fore he pulled out. In the course of his mining he uncovered the coal veins."

"Sounds reasonable," admitted Lank, "but what good is the coal to us? We don't need it to make fires of, and carrying coal fifty miles to town is too much of a chore and wouldn't pay."

Old Tom gloomily nodded agreement to Mason's pessimistic words, but Huck Brannon's eyes still glowed with enthusiasm.

Huck was thinking of the words of the C. & P. wreck-train foreman, spoken as the long coal drags rumbled past the siding:

"No mines in this district, and you gotta have fuel to keep a railroad goin'. Coal bill for the Mountain Division is jest 'bout double, mebbe more, what it costs on any other division."

Huck repeated the words now to his partners. "Don't you see?" the cowpuncher went on. "There's a wide-open market for all the coal we can mine. And we won't have to pack it to town, either. The railroad will run a spur up here, once we show them what we got. There's an easy water-level route up the river and the creek. All we got to do is locate our claims and open up our mine."

"Takes money," Lank said dubiously.

"I got some," said Old Tom. "Coupla thousand dollars put 'way."

"And I got 'nother thousand, mebbe a little more," Lank admitted.

They turned their eyes to Huck, whose brow was furrowed.

"Three thousand dollars," he mused. "With another five thousand, we could get the machinery we need and start producing. I haven't got the five thousand, boys, but I believe I can get it, with the security we have to offer. Do you want to risk your three thousand on that chance?"

Old Tom shrugged bony shoulders. " 'Pears like our silver 'spectations has gone up the flume," he said. "Me, I don't like to pack a lickin' this way. I'm willin' to take a chanct."

"Me, too," Lank grunted. "It's liable to all go in a poker game sooner or later, anyhow. So why not?"

He sniffed speculatively and eyed the pinkish

glow inside the lamp gauze. "She'll be a blazer, though," he predicted. "Gotta have a good blower system operatin' to pull the gas out, onct we start bringin' down the coal. Gas explosion in a coal mine ain't no picnic, friends."

Huck nodded with emphasis. "Let's fill a sack with samples," he said. "We'll try some out on our cookin' fire and take the rest to town with us."

A few minutes later they were trudging toward the main gallery. Huck and Lank paused from time to time to examine the walls of the side tunnel and to chart the course of the vein mentally. Old Tom got well ahead of them, reached the main corridor while they were still far behind. But his sudden howl brought them toward him at a gallop.

"It's one of them damn corpses from the cave!" Old Tom bawled. "I seed him lookin' 'round the corner and then he jest dis'peared!"

"Corpse, hell!" growled Brannon, dashing down the corridor.

He caught a glimpse of a denser shadow flitting through the ring of radiance cast by his lamp, and his hand streaked to his gun. There was a *crack,* a spurt of hot fire from the darkness; and Huck's knees buckled. He sprawled motionless on the rocky floor of the shaft. His lamp clattered on the floor and went out.

XIII

A Big Dream

Shouting and cursing, Mason and Old Tom ran to him. He groaned and stirred as they knelt beside him, and Lank opened Huck's shirt to feel for the heartbeat.

"Jest creased, the Lord be praised!" Old Tom muttered, pointing to a welling of blood at the hairline above one bronzed temple.

A moment later Huck opened his eyes, stared dazedly about and shook his head to clear it. The fog lifted from his brain, and he sat up slowly.

"The hellion shot at my lamp," he said, picking up his fallen cap and showing the jagged tear just below where the lamp hooked to the supporting bracket. "Mighty good shooting, too," he added, getting to his feet. "Gents, somebody's taking a powerful interest in what we're doing. Begins to look like somebody knows about you having that map, Tom."

"Don't know who it could be," said Gaylord, shaking his grizzled head. "I shore never showed it to nobody 'ceptin' you fellers."

"All right, boys," said Huck clambering to his

feet. His strength was returning and he felt less shaken. "Let's get back to the camp. We want to make sure the varmint hasn't cleaned us out."

With alacrity they complied, and with Lank leading the way, holding his lamp high, the three men hurried down the corridor of the main tunnel and emerged from the mine.

A quick survey of their gear revealed that this time no one had tampered with it.

Old Tom dubiously shook his head.

"Can't say as I like it nohow," he said. "Mebbe them dead Injuns in there"—he nodded in the direction of the mine—"have set a cuss on the mine to pr'tect their grave."

"I don't take much stock in curses, Tom," Huck said, kneeling to light a match to the fire. "Besides, one certain thing is that the lad who creased me is no ghost. Ghosts don't leave foot-prints and shoot guns." He leaned back. The fire was spreading around the pit.

"Mebbe it warn't a ghost," Old Tom persisted, "but yuh know how Injuns like to keep tradition alive. They hand it down from gen'ration to gen'ration, from father to son, an' it becomes part of their religion. Mebbe this is one of their sacred places."

"Yeah," agreed Lank Mason from across the fire, "mebbe it's like Tom says, Huck. I heard of them things, an' they're shore pow'ful when they get loose. If we're gonna buck one of them taboos, there's gonna be all hell let loose 'round here."

"Let's not invent trouble," said Huck, "Indian or any other kind. In the first place, one Indian isn't a tribe, and a lone brave is no sign there's a taboo on the mine. In the second place, we don't know yet if we're going to be here long." He took some lumps of the coal from the sack and held them in his hands. "But we'll find out soon enough. Then we'll cross our bridges—if we come to any." He hunkered thoughtfully down on his haunches and tossed the coals one by one into the fire.

The black, jagged lumps hit the flame with a sizzle and a small shower of sparks spurted upward. Their eyes intent, their bodies unconsciously stiffened and bent slightly forward, the partners gazed with deep concentration on the little rim of fire that held their future in its dancing, brilliant fingers.

For a while, they heard no sound but the crackling of the fire underneath the coals. Then Old Tom gulped noisily and Lank Mason swore under his breath. Huck remained silent.

Finally Old Tom could not longer hold his tongue. "It's burnin'!" he cried. "It's burnin'!"

"Yeah!" Lank Mason said vociferously. "It's burnin' coal, a'right."

The black, misshapen lumps, set like diamonds in their ring of fire, were by now themselves enkindled, casting steady intense blue-white flame skyward.

The three men looked at each other and grinned.

"It looks like the real stuff," Huck said, grin-wrinkles quirking the corners of his eyes and mouth. "I'm pretty sure we've got something here."

"Fust thing we gotta do," cried Mason, practical-minded, "is to hightail it back to town an stake our claim."

"First thing we gotta do," Huck said, "is to get some food into our bellies, so we don't collapse."

The odor of frying bacon and sausages and fresh coffee steaming rose from the fire, the pans rattling in Lank Mason's big hands. In ten minutes the food had disappeared.

They stretched back lazily, relaxing and letting their day dreams stray. Lank and Huck got their makings out and began rolling cigarettes as Old Tom spoke his dream.

"I allus figgered," he said, "that if I ever struck it rich I would like to travel an' see the world. Ever since I can remember, even when I was a kid, I wanted to see how the other feller works an' lives."

Lank Mason blew a whirl of cigarette smoke into the air before he spoke.

"Don't laugh at me," he said, "but the thing I allus wanted most, was"—he hesitated and looked cagily at his companions before he continued—"a chicken farm. Yep. I growed up on one an' I reckon I got poultry-handlin' in my blood. There ain't nothing purtier to my mind than a white chicken." And he chuckled aloud and there came to his eyes, half-hidden in the folds of pink flesh, a soft, dreamy glint.

"An' what yuh hankerin' for, Huck?" Tom Gaylord inquired.

"Well," Huck began slowly, "maybe it's too early to start sprouting dreams, but I always wanted to have me a place of my own, stocked full of fancy-bred cattle. My father had it and lost it. I want a good stretch of grassland with plenty of water, ravines and gullies to winter my stock. I want a good hoss under me. And—" His voice drifted away.

"Say, what's eatin' yuh?" cried Mason, staring at the puncher.

Huck was leaning on an elbow, staring into the fire. His attention had plainly strayed from the talk to some secret thought of his own. He looked sheepishly up at the question and his easy laughter was half apologetic.

"I'm sorry, fellows," he said shamefacedly, "I reckon I was wool-gatherin'."

"Say, what's come over yuh lately, Huck?" Mason demanded. " 'Pears to me yuh got that far-away look on yore face ev'ry time I look at yuh."

"Nothing," Huck replied quickly. "It's nothing."

"Nothin', huh?" Old Tom said shrewdly. "Nothin' my foot." He winked at Mason. "I bet yuh a barrel of coal, outa that mine of our'n, Huck's moonin' over some gal."

Huck laughed, but the sound was a dead give-away.

"Ha!" Lank Mason shouted. "So it *is* a gal. Why, yuh onery, double-crossin', lovesick maverick. Castin' aside yore pardners for some ol' gal. Out with it, hombre. Who is this here dream that's gonna rob us of our side kick?"

With a laugh, Huck confessed there was a girl, but no amount of persuasion could induce him to say any more.

"C'mon, boys," Huck said after a moment. "We got work ahead of us."

"I'm still wonderin'," said Mason as they broke camp and prepared to leave, "where that foot-print came from, and who took a shot at Huck?"

Could the partners, making their way back to town, have looked into the back room of a dis-reputable little saloon in Esmeralda, they would have found the solution of the mystery.

Cale Coleman was there, in his hand the cane he hobbled about on. There also was his shifty-eyed drift-foreman, Jeff Eades.

The third member of an unsavory trio was a swarthy, undersized man, wiry and long of arm. His eyes were dead black, his hair lank and stringy. Yellowish-coppery skin was drawn tightly over high cheekbones and the eyes were set deep in their sockets. His mouth was a thin red line from which frequently protruded the tip of a tongue that flickered like a snake's as it moistened the too-thin, too-red lips. His voice had the harsh guttural tone and his accents the clipped terseness of the Indian-Latin.

"Well, what the hell'd you find out, Estaban?" Coleman demanded. "What'd the hellions do?"

"Blowed up crick," grunted the halfbreed.

Coleman let out a roar and his blocky face suffused with red.

"You tryin' to be funny?" he demanded. "What the blankety-blank-blank you talkin' 'bout? 'Blowed up a crick'!"

"Blowed up crick, make water run down hill, show topside up hole in cliff where waterfall come down, go in hole," replied the halfbreed.

Coleman showed all the signs of an explosion, but Jeff Eades hastened to interpret.

"You mean they changed the course of the crick and found a cave back of where the falls come down?"

Estaban nodded. "No cave," he said. "Mine tunnel."

"Mine tunnel!" barked Coleman. "What the devil—"

"Tunnel there long time," grunted Estaban. "Damn old. Somebody cover up with water— long time."

Coleman's eyes blazed with excitement. "A lost mine, Jess, shore as anything!" he exclaimed. "Them hellions musta knowed somethin'!"

He whirled to the halfbreed. "What'd they find?" he demanded. "What'd they do?"

"Fill um sack with black rocks," replied Estaban.

His listeners stared at him. "Black rocks," repeated Coleman. "Gold—silver?"

Estaban shook his head. "Nope, black rocks—heap shine."

Coleman swore helplessly. "The damn igner'nt Injun!" he spat.

"What'd they do then, Estaban?" Eades prompted.

"Me no know," said the halfbreed. "They see, chase. Me shoot one. Come 'way—damn fast!"

"They see who you was, you blankety-blank clumsy blankety-blank?" demanded Coleman, raising the heavy cane threateningly.

The halfbreed did not change countenance under the menace of the bludgeon, but his beady eyes glowed a little and one sinewy hand crept closer to the heavy gun thrust under his belt.

Coleman saw the gesture and although his eyes remained murderous he lowered the cane.

"No see in the dark," said Estaban. "They think me one of watchers that sit in dark and look without eyes. Me come 'way fast."

That was all they could get out of him.

"I jest hope it was that damn black-haided hellion he plugged, anyway," growled Coleman. "You keep outa sight in case they did get a glim of you," he told the halfbreed. "Jeff, you keep yore eyes open for them headin' back inter town. We gotta find out what they was lookin' for and what they found, if anythin'. Have one of the boys hang 'round the assay office. That's where they'll head for if they've hit onto any ore. Then if we find they found anythin' interestin', we'll move fast."

Eades stared at him. "You ain't figgerin' on any claim jumpin', are you? There's things even *you* can't get by with, Cale, and claim jumpin' in a minin' country's one of 'em. A killin' and robbin' now and then, yeah, and even some hoss stealin', mebbe, but bust minin' laws and you'll have a vig'lance committee waitin' on you."

Coleman turned his gaze on his foreman and his eyes were cold and calculating.

"You don't hafta *jump* a claim filed by dead men," he said softly.

XIV

From Texas

On reaching town, Huck learned that General-Manager Dunn had arrived at Esmeralda the day before. He wasted no time in going to Dunn's office. He sent in his name and was admitted without delay.

The empire-builder greeted him cordially, a pleased gleam beading his frosty eyes.

"Well, son—decided to go into railroading?" he asked. "Looking for a job?"

Huck smiled down at him from his great height. "No, sir," he disclaimed. "I'm here to sell you something."

"Something to sell?" Dunn said, his eyes on the sack Huck carried.

Dunn's desk was extremely wide, with a massive flat glass top. There was very little on the top aside from papers neatly stacked near his right hand.

On the shimmering surface beside the documents, Huck put down several of his irregular black lumps. Jaggers Dunn stared at them in astonishment.

126

"You been robbing cars out in the yards?" he demanded at last.

Huck Brannon grinned. "I've a notion," he replied, "that you haven't anything just like it in any of your coal cars. Take a good look at it."

Jaggers Dunn did, puckering his shaggy white brows, peering narrowly with his frosty blue eyes. He rubbed one of the lumps on a clean sheet of white paper and examined the faint smudge left by the contact.

"Semi-bituminous," Huck heard him mutter incredulously. "Almost cannel coal. Mighty near as dustless as anthracite!"

He fixed the cowboy with a piercing gaze. "This what you got to sell?" he demanded.

Huck nodded.

"Shoot!" said the empire-builder.

Huck told him about it tersely.

"I've a notion," he added, "that the day'll come when this Colorado country will be a lot better known for coal than it ever was for gold or silver. Such seams as crop out in those tunnels aren't just freak veins. I'm willing to bet my last peso that a big field underlies this whole section.

"I noticed outcroppings of limestone and sandstone between here and the canyon, and in the canyon itself, which is more evidence of the presence of coal hereabouts."

Dunn listened with absorbed interest, turning

127

over a lump of the coal in his big fingers. When the cowboy had finished, he asked several precise and to-the-point questions, nodding his white head to each reply.

"Looks good," he admitted at length. "You're sure the veins are thick enough to permit of profitable working?"

"My recollection is that six feet is considered an excellent working thickness in the Pennsylvania mines," Huck replied. "We've got close to ten feet. Looks like rumpled seams and may need a shaft for the best results before we get going good, but the tunnels already driven for us will do in the beginning. We'll use the panel system in getting the coal out, I figger."

"You're properly located and filed?"

"Here are the papers, sir. I figure you'll find them correct."

"All right. I'll send an engineering party to look over the ground. If their report is favorable, you can start operations at once. The road will run a spur to the mine, and we'll buy every lump you produce, at current market prices."

His stern face lighted as he shook hands with the cowboy, and his smile was wonderfully youthful.

"I want to see you succeed, son," he said. "What this country needs is men who believe in it, who can dream, and make their dreams come true."

With the promise of the general-manager still ringing in his ears, Huck left the office, his head busy and spinning, his heart pounding. He strode down the main street and his lips formed a thin, straight line of determination.

Here was his chance to get all the things he'd ever wanted. The things worth fighting for. The range he wanted; the cattle he wanted, the girl he'd dreamed of. Especially the girl. He had been fighting to shut her completely from his mind. Now there was no longer any need.

Perhaps in a short time he would be able to take a train to Stevens Gulch and pay her a visit. He smiled dreamily at the thought. In his complete absorption, he became completely oblivious to the rest of the street. His first inkling that he was not utterly alone came when:

"Why don'tcha look where yuh're goin'?" a voice cried in his face.

Huck brought up short in the arms of the man he had nearly bowled over. He looked like a miner. He shot Huck a murderous glance.

"Sorry," Huck muttered, and strode on.

Ahead of him lay his destination—the telegraph office. He entered and asked the clerk for a form. He walked to the writing table, sat down, picked up the pencil and began to compose his telegram.

"Mr. Wyatt Doyle, the Bar X Ranch," he wrote, "Stevens Gulch, Texas." The pencil faltered.

How could he ask Doyle for a loan when he was in love with Sue? It didn't seem right. Yet he had every reason to expect that Doyle would grant the loan. Huck's father had been Doyle's close friend. And Doyle had always treated Huck pretty much like his own son. Moreover, Huck was offering what he knew to be good security—his share of the coal mine.

Of course it would mean an alteration in his relationship to Sue. The loan would have to be paid off first, before he would permit himself to think of her at all. He didn't want to court Sue while he was under any kind of obligation to her father. His heart rebelled, but his mind told him that he was acting as he must. After all, he had an obligation to his partners, too.

The pencil moved again. Huck wrote rapidly, and was soon finished. Before signing his name, he added another phrase, but not without hesitation. Then he crossed it out. Once more he wrote it in. Again he crossed it out.

He left it that way, and gave the message to the operator.

"I reckon," he said to himself as he stepped out of the door, "that I'll have to hold on to my regards to Sue for a while yet."

He picked up Mason and Old Tom where he had left them—at the saloon. Then he and his partners got busy.

They rented a little shack to use as an office

and Huck put in orders for the necessary mining machinery, making a down payment from the three thousand dollars provided by Mason and Gaylord, the balance to be paid on delivery. The question of labor came up.

"I know a few rock-busters I can get," said Lank Mason. "Fellers I worked with on Coleman's diggin's. They ain't over hankerin' to stay on with that galoot if they can get somethin' else to do in the district. They'll be glad to throw in with us. There's five good men I know of who can handle foreman's work if nec'sary."

"Offer them a stake in the mine, too," suggested Huck. "That'll hold them on the job. A man gets interested in a job when he sees something more coming to him than just wages."

The others nodded.

"When it comes to pick and shovel men, feller, you got me stumped," said Lank. " 'Pears we're gonna hafta send outa the district, and that's 'spensive. 'Sides, the sorta gandy-dancers you get that-away is allus on the move. Work till they get a stake and then shove on."

Huck suggested: "There's lots of strong, willing men over in the Mexican settlement west of town. They don't get so much chance in the mines around here—the hardest work and the poorest pay, and they're always the first to get laid off. I suggest we get together an outfit of hands from among the Mexes."

Lank was dubious. "I ain't never took much stock in greasers," he said.

"In the first place," Huck replied, "don't call them greasers. They don't like the name, and I don't blame 'em. So if they work for us, that name is out.

"In the second place, I *do* take stock in Mexicans. I've worked with them on ranches below the Line and in Texas and Arizona, and I always found them to come as good on the average as any other hands. If you treat 'em square and they like you, they'll go through hell and high water for you, and they never forget a favor."

"Reckon that's right," Tom Gaylord said. "Rec'lect it was that old Mexican feller I helped what give me the map. Him and his pals couldn't seem to do enough for me. They didn't have much, but I was plumb welcome to ev'thin' they did have. Tell you what, Huck, I sling their lingo purty nigh as well as you do, and I could allus get 'long with 'em. I'll jest mosey over to the settlement and see if I can't get together a crew."

In a few days the C. & P. engineers brought back a favorable report. Huck, who had gone ahead in full confidence in his own judgment, was gratified to have it substantiated by experts. Lank at once set out for the mine, taking his crew of rock-busters and pickmen with him. Huck smiled

132

happily as he watched the long, straggling train of men and mules vanish into the hills.

Old Tom, who was to have charge of the Esmeralda office and the numerous details demanding attention there, chuckled in his beard. Huck was staying on in Esmeralda until he received word from Texas and until the arrival of the machinery shipments.

There were neither smiles nor chuckles, however, in the back room of the saloon on the outskirts of town. Cale Coleman, his face black with rage, watched the mule train out of sight. Then he clumped to the table and sat down with a bitter curse.

The halfbreed Estaban had trailed the engineering party to their destination, but had known better than to attempt an attack on or approach too close to the strong and experienced railroad outfit. From a safe distance he watched them look over the mine and then he'd hastened back to report to Coleman.

Coleman, in the meanwhile, after a fruitless picketing of the assay office, had belatedly thought to ascertain if Huck and his partners had filed location papers. When he found out what was in the wind, it was too late to do anything about it.

Not that Coleman admitted defeat. He was too shrewd, too reckless of consequences, too utterly unscrupulous to give up so easily. He was the richest man in Esmeralda, owner of the most productive gold mines and president of the Esmeralda bank. And he hadn't achieved any of it by caution or hesitant half-measures.

"Let the blankety-blanks go ahaid and start op'rations," he told Jeff Eades. "Let 'em get things workin' good and then we'll move in on 'em. There's more ways of ketchin' a skunk than pourin' molasses on its tail. Right now I want you to do a little nosin' 'round in the Apishapa River Valley 'tween here and Dominguez Crick. Take Connolly and Bates with you—they're both from the Pennsylvania fields—and see what you can find out."

Eades hesitated a moment, then gave his boss some good advice:

"I figger that's the most sensible thing to do in the fust place. Ferget them three hellions and do some smart perspectin' on our own hook. That's the idea."

Coleman growled a curse, and tenderly shifted his bandaged leg. "I ain't fergettin' anythin'," he told the drift-foreman venomously. "When I start out to even up things with a hellion, I finish what I start."

"That big jigger's a cold prop'sition, boss," objected Eades dubiously.

"He'll be colder still when I get through with him," Coleman replied with significant emphasis.

Eades turned to leave when the hard voice of his boss stopped him.

"Eades," Coleman growled, "send Estaban back in here. I got a special job for the half-breed—yeah, a very special job."

"Okay, Coleman," said Eades.

Cale Coleman stared at the door which his foreman, Jeff Eades, had just closed behind him. His black eyes glittered in an otherwise cold and controlled face—a face that gave an unmistakable impression of cruelty and passionless calculation.

The thin straight line of his lips began to curl, his jet black eyebrows arched slightly and the pupils of his eyes dilated, almost imperceptibly.

"I'll fix that hombre," he muttered to himself. He almost snarled as the image of Huck Brannon appeared before him.

Ever since Huck Brannon had subjected him, Cale Coleman, the biggest and richest man in Esmeralda, to a public beating, which had put him in the hospital with a broken leg, he had been determined on paying Brannon back.

No man had ever stood up against him and come out on top. But more to the point was that no one had ever subjected him to such public ridicule and gnawing humiliation. His vanity had been mortally wounded, his pride stung.

And now, adding to the flames, was the fact that this young hellion had apparently struck it rich in a territory which he, Cale Coleman, had always considered his own exclusive property.

His long, thin fingers beat a rapid tattoo on the table as he waited fretfully for Estaban. His mind had hatched a plan—a cunning plan which would effectively rid him of the annoying presence of Huck Brannon.

Estaban would do the job, all right. And if the halfbreed raised any objections, he had a means of reminding him that the job *ought* to be carried out. No, he didn't anticipate any trouble with Estaban. But where the devil *was* he?

Estaban was somber and inscrutable when he entered a few moments later. His eyes were as black and glittering as the man's he faced, and even more impenetrable.

"Coleman send?" His voice was as blank as his face.

"Yeah, blast it!" the big boss of Esmeralda roared, his impatience exploding. "Where the hell were you?"

"Estaban outside," answered the halfbreed quietly, showing no sign of fear.

Coleman subsided when he saw that his temper had little visible effect on the breed.

"I have another job for yuh," he said sullenly.

"Coleman know Estaban do," the ochre-faced man answered.

This immediate obedience had a gratifying effect on Coleman; his eyes lighted up and he smiled, showing his teeth wolfishly.

"Now listen—" he began and bent forward slightly as he swiftly outlined his plan to the Indian. In a few minutes he had finished, and he glanced up into his companion's face, expecting to see approval there. Instead he found Estaban shaking his head in the negative.

"What's the matter now?" demanded Coleman.

"Estaban no do," said the half-breed.

"Why not?" Coleman roared.

"Estaban no do," the Indian repeated stubbornly.

"You'll do it, all right," snarled Coleman. "Don't forget there's a place up North that's waiting for you—" It wasn't necessary for him to continue.

Estaban's face, underneath its coppery hue, went yellowish white. The tip of his tongue slithered out and licked his dry, cracked lips. He seemed to gulp for air. When he spoke, it was a bare, hoarse whisper.

"Estaban do," he croaked.

"I knew I could depend on you," Coleman crowed, triumphantly.

XV

Reunion

Impatiently, like a thoroughbred champing at the bit, Sue Doyle paced the wood-boarded station at Kansas City waiting for the train that would take her back to Stevens Gulch. To the Bar X Ranch she had left almost six weeks ago.

In her right hand, crumpled and wrinkled, was clenched a telegram which she nervously smoothed out and reread for the hundredth time. Again her hand jolted to her side and she resumed her nervous pacing, craning her neck from time to time to see if the train was in sight.

Almost six weeks had elapsed since Sue Doyle had set out in search of Huck Brannon, and a long, long time it seemed. Yet there was no change in her appearance. She was still the same long-limbed, amber-eyed, black-haired girl. Even steady disappointment had not been able to dim her radiance.

And she had been steadily disappointed until she returned to Kansas City and found the telegram from her father, waiting. That had set her feverishly stalking the platform. What a fool she'd been!

Acting on the opinion of the yardmaster that Chuck had headed East, she had boarded the first train in that direction and began a fruitless, aimless search. It had taken her through three states, to an endless number of ranches, to mines and sometimes to saloons.

It had all been a waste of time. Not a single station master, nor rancher, nor mine foreman, nor saloonkeeper could definitely remember seeing a tall, black-haired, gray-eyed, well-knit Arizona cowpoke. A few thought they recognized the description and had added fuel to the flame of hope in Sue's breast. But not once did she get a really definite lead. All hope had ended in failure. She shook her head as she remembered disappointment after disappointment.

She had begun to despair of ever finding trace of Huck. But she had persisted and run every lead, no matter how ambiguous, to the ground. It had never occurred to her to give up the search. Then she had decided one day that perhaps it was the yardmaster who had given her the wrong steer. Perhaps she should have headed West, rather than East. Maybe Huck had jumped a freight going in the opposite direction.

This thought had preyed on her mind, until she decided to start from the beginning again— at Kansas City—and go West. It was quite possible, she had reflected, that the yardmaster had been wrong.

Acting quickly on her decision she had taken the first train back to Kansas City. But she had not neglected to send a wire to her father advising him of her change of direction.

Arriving in Kansas City, she found a telegram addressed to her. She stopped pacing, for she just heard the engine's whistle. It was finally coming. Once more she smoothed out the yellowish piece of paper in her hand. It read:

DEAR SUE. COME HOME. FOUND YOUR MAN.
    LOVE.   FATHER

Swiftly the days passed. Lank reported progress from the mine. With amazing speed, Jaggers Dunn's railroad builders shoved a line of track up the valley of the Apishapa. Dunn himself delayed an important trip East to supervise the work.

"Getting this coal right here on the Mountain Division will mean a saving to the road that can't be estimated," he told Huck Brannon. "We'll be ready to shove your machinery a good ways up the valley by the time it arrives in Esmeralda. The boys are doing a fine job of work and not encountering any trouble."

Huck Brannon, however, *was* encountering trouble. Day after day passed, and no word from Texas.

"I was plumb shore Wyatt Doyle, who owns the

Bar X, would lend me the five thousand, under the circumstances," he complained to Gaylord. "I worked for Doyle, you know. Doyle and my dad were mighty close friends back in the old days. Dad and he rode together in Arizona and New Mexico.

"Then Dad got married and Doyle shoved off into Texas, but they always kept track of each other. Old Ah Sing, Doyle's Chinese cook, used to work for Dad before he lost his spread. Ah Sing just about raised me after Mom passed on when I was six or thereabouts. When our spread busted up, Ah Sing went to the Bar X. He saved Doyle's life one day, too."

"How's that, Huck?"

"Well, a passel of wideloopers rode up to the Bar X one day when the boys were all in town. They come looking for Doyle, him having hung a couple of their pals when he was deputy sheriff. They got the drop on him and started out to string him up. Decided to fill their bellies first, though, and set Ah Sing to rustling together a big kettle of stew."

Huck paused to roll a quirly.

"And—" Old Tom prompted.

"And, Ah Sing emptied some strychnine he'd been using to poison wolves into the stew."

"Cute feller!"

"Uh-huh, he is. Doyle told me he got almighty tired burying wideloopers that day."

Gaylord shook his head sadly. "Awful waste o' labor!" he commented. "Looks like Doyle woulda answered yore telegram, anyhow."

"Uh-huh, that's what I thought. Well, it sure seems like I'll have to try to get the dinero from the bank; and I figure they'll charge me plenty for it."

"Uh-huh, puhlenty!" Gaylord agreed dryly. "I un'stan' that feller Coleman, the one you walloped the waddin' outa, jest 'bout owns the bank. I reckon he won't want more'n a half-interest in the mine!"

"Whe-e-e-e-ew!" Huck stared at his partner. "You sure of that?"

Gaylord nodded somberly.

"And that machinery is due day after tomorrow!" Huck growled. "Tom, I gotta do some figuring!"

He was still figuring, with a jumble of figures that refused to come out right, the next day when Old Tom entered the office.

"Feller out here wants to see you—Chinese feller," said Gaylord.

"I already gave my washing to the one across the street," grunted Huck, frowning over his pencil.

"Mebbe he's finished with it and's deliverin' it," suggested Gaylord. "He's got a big sack."

"All right," Huck sighed, fumbling in his pockets. "Send him in."

Still staring at the paper before him, he heard slippered feet slither across the rough floor. He turned absently, and then leaped to his feet, his overturned chair crashing to the floor.

Across the desk were peering two beady black eyes set aslant in a yellow, wrinkled old face. The owner of eyes and face showed a line of gums in a toothless grin.

"H'lo, Huck," he said in a voice like a rusty hinge. "Belly cold t'day, belly cold!"

After a moment of goggle-eyed astonishment, Huck found his voice.

"You yellow heathen!" he exclaimed, pump-handling the old Chinaman's withered claw. "How many times have I told you if you'd tuck your shirt inside your pants like decent folks, your belly wouldn't be cold! Where in blazes did you come from?"

Old Ah Sing, the Bar X cook, chuckled as he always did at that ancient joke about his inability to properly pronounce v's and r's.

"Me come flom Texas," he said.

"So I figure," Huck agreed. "But what are you doing way up here?"

"You f'glet clothes when you no come back from Kansas City," Ah Sing replied. "Me bling!"

He heaved a bulging sack to the top of the desk and loosened the pucker string. While Huck stared at him in slack-jawed amazement, he produced riding breeches, shiny high-heeled boots, well-worn shotgun chaps, shirts, silk handker-chiefs, a much crumpled Stetson broad of brim and dimpled of crown, and finally two long-barreled Colts with plain, serviceable handles and snugged into carefully worked and oiled cut-out holsters attached to a well filled home-made double cartridge belt.

Huck stared at the "workin' " clothes that had come back to him after this considerable period.

"Old Man send," said Ah Sing.

"You mean to tell me Old Man Doyle sent you all the way up here with my outfit?" demanded the amazed cowboy.

"Can do," admitted Ah Sing. He fumbled in the flattened sack and drew forth a securely wrapped package.

"Send this too," he observed, laying it on the desk.

"What's that?" wondered Huck.

"Fi' thousand dollas—you count," Ah Sing said blandly.

Dazedly Huck ripped open the package and exposed the stack of big bills.

"Oh, my gosh!" Old Tom Gaylord gurgled. "Send a Chinaman all the way from Texas with five thousand dollars in a sack of clothes!"

"Safe!" observed Ah Sing. "Nobody steal old clothes!"

"Reckon that's right," Gaylord admitted. "Feller, you ain't no fool."

"No," agreed Ah Sing, "me cook."

"Five thousand is correct," said Huck, glancing up with shining eyes. "How is the Old Man—and everybody, Ah Sing?"

"Ev'body fine," said the Chinaman.

Huck hesitated, then asked another question.

"How—how's Sue—an' Smoke? Smoke was my pet cuttin' hoss," he explained to Gaylord. "I set a heap of store by Smoke."

Ah Sing chuckled again. "You come outside," he invited.

Wondering, Huck obeyed. He stopped short at the door and for the third time stared in almost unbelief.

Standing by the stoop, complete with silver stamped bridle and huge Mexican saddle, was a tall horse of a peculiar gray-blue color.

His horse, Smoke. But what was more astounding and breathtaking to Huck, was that sitting straight-backed in the saddle—was Sue! Sue Doyle!

Huck blinked helplessly at Sue, who was smiling across at him; consciously he took a deep breath and his cheeks puckered and lips pursed.

"Hello, Huck." Sue's voice seemed to float from a great distance.

"Sue!" he cried, with a sharp intake of breath.

He was dimly aware of a heavy pulse pounding in his ears, and of a giddy lightheartedness that suddenly came to him. Then he galvanized into action.

He took the steps three at a time and passed Smoke, who stretched his glossy neck and wickered plaintively at the sight of the cowboy.

But for once Huck was impervious to the sight of his horse. It was the girl *on* the horse who held his attention.

Sue had slipped out of the saddle as he came down the steps and now Huck took her in his arms, almost without realizing what he was doing, and kissed her hard on the lips.

"Sue, darling," he heard a voice say. It sounded like his own.

Almost in a daze he felt her respond, and heard her whisper:

"Huck, dear." Then he heard her laugh. "Let me down, Huck," she was saying. "Everyone is looking at us."

Slowly he let her slide out of his arms, a red, tell-tale flush burning into his cheeks. He turned to find Lank Mason, Old Tom and Ah Sing grinning down at him from the porch. They made no pretense of hiding their delighted and rapt interest in the proceedings.

Embarassedly, Huck introduced his partners and friends to Sue Doyle. They eyed her with immediate approval; and with Old Tom, the swift approval grew to almost a fatherly fondness.

"So this here is the gal yuh been moonin'

over," cried Mason gleefully, a smile cutting his face. "Wal—I reckon I can't say's I blame yah. No sir, by heck—makes we wish I was twenty years younger myself."

"Hold yore tongue, Mason," Old Tom cried with pretended indignation. "What's none of yore bus'ness is none of yore bus'ness."

"I'm starved," said Sue, relieving the situation for Huck, who was growing redder by the minute.

"C'mon, Lank," said Old Tom. "We got a million things to attend to. Huck, why don't yuh take Miss Doyle to the restaurant? Yuh heard her say she's starvin'? 'Pears to me if I heard a young lady—an' a right purty one, too—say she's hungry—I'd know what to do."

Huck shook his head dazedly. He still couldn't believe that Sue had come all the way out here to join him, and he was afraid to trust the obvious interpretation of her act. He couldn't think of a thing to say or do except to follow Old Tom's advice, and take Sue to a restaurant.

Before he did that, however, he answered the appeal in the luminous eyes of his horse, Smoke, whom he had almost forgotten until this moment. He stroked the gracefully arched neck; and in gratefulness, the big horse thrust a velvet muzzle into his hand and snorted his pleasure.

Matt Bird's restaurant, the cleanest in Esmeralda, was virtually deserted when Huck and Sue entered. Now, seated opposite one another, eating the well-cooked meal Huck had ordered and Matt himself had served, Sue was chattering happily. And if she noticed any gaps in Huck's conversation, she did not comment on it.

It was a strange silence that had paralyzed Huck's tongue, so that he merely sat and gazed at the face he saw was flushed and lovely looking.

"I was mighty surprised to see you, Sue," he said.

"Well," she returned, "you don't think Father was going to make a loan without sending someone to see to it that his interests were protected."

"But I sent him my share in the mine, as security," Huck protested.

"Of course you did, Huck," said Sue. "Nevertheless, Dad wanted to make certain his money was used properly. So I came as his representative to make sure." She laughed aloud as she saw his face darkening. "Oh, you're such a goose, Huck. You know Dad would trust you without any security. As a matter of fact, he told me to give you back the assignment on your mine that you sent him."

"Thanks." Huck's gray eyes gleamed and the crowsfeet lines of a smile webbed the corners of his eyes as he accepted the paper Sue held out.

"I really came with Ah Sing to bring the money to you," Sue continued, "and besides,

Dad thought I needed a vacation. So here I am."

"But Smoke?" asked Huck. "How did you get him here?"

"We brought him in a box stall," replied Sue. "I thought you might need him."

"Don't figure I'll need him much up here," Huck said, "but I'm glad you brought him."

Little did Huck know that the time would soon come when he would need the big blue horse, and need him plenty!

When his tongue finally loosened, it was to ask about the Bar X Ranch. He hadn't realized until now how he hungered for information—about the boys, about Doyle, about the place. But all the time his eyes were fastened on her face.

Sue satisfied him on all counts and also casually mentioned that she had been to Kansas City some time ago and heard that he had gotten into a little scrape there.

"Yes," said Huck, his anxiety showing on his face. "I always wondered how that jigger I hit was doing. Always meant to find out, too, but I've been kinda busy—or maybe to tell the truth I just plumb forgot."

"You put him into the hospital for a couple of weeks," said Sue. "But he's all right now."

"That's fine," Huck said. "I'm powerful eased to hear it. I didn't want anybody's death on my conscience. . . . What's the matter, Sue?" He had noticed a look of puzzlement on her face.

"Nothing," she replied at once. "Nothing at all. Tell me about your mine, Huck."

So Huck launched into the story of the El Padre. He started from the beginning—of his first meeting with Old Tom and Lank Mason. He passed lightly over the episode of his rescue of the old man and went on to tell Sue of the job he had taken, of the scrap with Cale Coleman and finally of the search for and discovery of the lost mine.

He could see that she was keenly interested in the recital, and added that Old Tom feared there was a curse on El Padre. And he told her of finding a moccasined footprint and of someone shooting out his Davey light. He read concern on her face.

"Do you think there'll be any trouble, Huck?" she asked.

"I don't think so," he reassured her. "An' if there is, I reckon we can take care of it."

But if Huck Brannon had been vouchsafed a brief glance into the future, he would not have been so confident.

"Huck," asked Sue—she seemed to deliberate for a moment before asking the question. And it may have been accidental, but she seemed also to evade looking at him. "Why didn't you come back to the Bar X?"

Now it was Huck's turn to deliberate and hesitate before speaking. What could he tell her?

That he had left the Bar X Ranch because of her? Because he had been afraid of going soft on her—he a footloose cowboy and she his owner's daughter? But it *had* happened, anyway. He *had* gone soft on her.

"I reckon," he evaded, "that I was getting pretty tired of riding herd. And getting restless, too. I itched to see what was on the other side of the hill. So I thought it was high time I pulled my stakes and got going. I wound up here—in Esmeralda—part-owner of a coal mine."

Huck fancied he saw a look of disappointment pass over Sue's face.

"Is that what you want to be, Huck?" she asked, staring frankly into his eyes. "A mine owner?"

"Why not?" he demanded. "It's as good as being anything else—especially if it pays off."

It was a lie, he knew. But once he had started to lie, he found it difficult to stop. Moreover, he had to keep his story straight.

After having hired a room for Sue with the wife of Jagger Dunn's foreman, Huck made his way slowly down the main street to his office.

He cursed himself for being a fool. When he had sent the telegram to Doyle, he had deliberately omitted sending a message to Sue. He was asking for a loan, and until the loan could be paid back he had determined to forget about Sue completely.

And now, it was all mixed up. If she had only

151

stayed away until he had gotten the mine running and the loan repaid, he wouldn't be feeling sorry that he had kissed her. Not that he was sorry he kissed her—no, certainly not. But he *was* —damn it!

When he entered his office, he found it difficult to shut out a certain picture and concentrate on the work before him.

Sue Doyle had trouble falling asleep that night.

Her search was over—she had found Huck Brannon. She had been ecstatically happy when he took her in his arms and kissed her. The reason for her coming had been fulfilled. She now knew definitely what Huck would do when he saw her. She knew because he had already done it. He kissed her—and she had been idiotically happy.

That is, until Huck had taken her to the restaurant. There, something had happened to him. She saw it happen before her eyes. He had turned cold and hard suddenly. He no longer looked at her the way he did when he first saw her. As she thought of it now, her heart stiffened.

She had been sure—positive—of his feeling. Now she wasn't any longer. She had been happy —wildly—at first. Now the cold tentacles of fear clutched at her heart, fear that something—some insurmountable obstacle stood between them.

Sue Doyle was most miserable before she fell asleep that night.

XVI

"We Will Kill You, If We Can"

The ghost of grim old Don Fernando de Castro would have been hard put to recognize his silver mine when the sun of returning Spring melted the snows on the mountains and clothed the hillsides with myriad shades of green. Instead of silence broken only by the low thunder of falling water, the cry of the eagle and the scream of the stalking panther there was the whine and rumble of machinery, the crackle of locomotive exhausts, the screech of complaining wheels and the crash of steel on steel. Instead of the stainless blue of the arching sky, there were sullen clouds belching forth from stack and chimney.

Inside the mine there were also changes. Drawn by mules and rumbling along on narrow-gauge tracks were trains of little cars heaped high with glistening black lumps. In the rooms cut back from the main galleries there was a thumping of picks and a pounding of drills, with ever and anon the rumble of explosions.

A deep shaft had been sunk within the mine and there were levels beneath the original borings. Cages raised and lowered by cables sent men into the lower levels and brought them forth. Other lifts brought forth the black diamonds torn from the heart of the mountain. There was a constant whistling of blowers that pumped the inflammable gas from the mine.

For the Lost Padre was a dangerous mine. It was, as Lank had predicted, a "blazer." Always present was the threat of an explosion that would leave death and destruction in its wake. Smoking was forbidden inside the mine and only the Davey safety lamps were used to provide illumination. Quite different from the smoking torches used by the doomed Indians who got out the silver for Don Fernando de Castro and His Imperial and Holy Majesty of Spain.

Only one thing was unchanged. Within their night-black tomb, the silence of which was broken only by the monotonous drip and trickle of water, the murdered Indians slept undisturbed their last long sleep. Huck Brannon had thought at first to remove the bodies and give them burial, but Tom Gaylord counseled against it.

"Our Mexican fellers is mighty superstitious," said Tom. "I got a notion they wouldn't take over-kindly to shovin' them corpses 'round. Fact is, I cal'late it's best if they don't even know they're in there."

"Maybe you're right," Huck admitted. "Lank,

take your rock-busters in there and throw up a wall across the gallery that leads into the cave where those poor devils are. Let 'em rest in peace where they been all these years."

So a light stone wall was built across the gallery from floor to ceiling. A shallow conduit with an arching top was constructed beneath the wall at one side, so that the seeping of water could be carried off.

"That's fine," Lank Mason observed, eyeing the completed wall with satisfaction. "That'll keep the boys outa there and from gettin' the livin' blue blazin' daylights scairt outa them. Fact is, I been hearin' things already. There's a whisper goin' around in town that this mine has a cuss on it, and that the Injuns what live back in the hills is mighty put out over us startin' operations here again.

"The Injuns say, I'm told, that this mine should stay closed forever and forever. They say it'll be a mighty bad thing for the red people if anythin' is taken outa the mountain again—say the hill gods'll be mad 'bout it. They figger the hill gods'll blame them if they don't stop it."

"Now who's starting those yarns?" demanded Huck.

"Dunno," Lank admitted. "They jest start; but they shore spread."

Sue joined them. She overheard Mason.

"What's sure to spread, Lank?" she asked him.

"Why, nothing, Sue—nothing," replied Huck quickly. "Lank was talking about some gas in the lower chambers. Said it was sure to spread if we didn't keep the blowers goin'."

For a moment Sue eyed him without saying a word, and she colored slightly. "Huck," she said calmly, "you're still treating me like a little girl. I know what's going on. There's talk of a curse on El Padre."

"Yes," Huck said. "Some blame fool's spreading the yarn. There isn't a word of truth to it. I just didn't want you to worry is all."

"It doesn't worry me, Huck," said Sue.

"Say," Lank interpolated. "I gotta hand it to yuh women. I ain't had meals like them since I was knee high to a pup. Why, since yuh came to stay at El Padre to do the cookin', I ain't heard a peep outa any of the men 'bout hard work, or nothin'!"

Sue blushed warmly at the praise.

"Thanks, Lank," she said.

When Sue Doyle had first come to Esmeralda, a short time back, she had no idea that she would soon become assistant camp cook for Huck Brannon at his El Padre Mine.

Yet it had come about in the most natural way in the world. The wife of Jagger Dunn's foreman, with whom Sue roomed when she arrived, was a robust, bustling Irishwoman, named Mamie Donovan. Bristling with an over-supply of vitality and energy, she had suggested to Huck at the opening of his mine, that she join his camp as cook.

Huck, immediately perceiving the advantage of obtaining the services of Mamie Donovan—for her cooking prowess was too well-known for dispute—hired her on the spot.

The good Mrs. Donovan immediately hired as assistant Sue Doyle, whom she had taken wholeheartedly to her more than ample bosom. And although Huck had at first protested at Sue's being on location, on the grounds that it was too dangerous for her, he finally had gratefully accepted her presence.

Sue, after the first shock of disappointment had worn off following the change in Huck's attitude toward her, had determined to stick it out—for a while at least—and had wired her father. Her pride was trampled and sore, but she refused to indulge it.

Lank and Old Tom, who had observed the situation with knowing eyes, had diagnosed the symptoms and read the chart accurately, were at a loss to understand their partner's reactions. Their oblique comments, however, had been cut short by Huck, who brooked no invasion of his privacy—and minced no words in making it clear to them.

Naturally, the oldsters' sympathies lay with the feminine side of the apparently insoluble equation. And in revenge for Huck's blistering tongue, they constantly praised Sue, extolled her virtues, her character, her beauty, to the very skies. And revenge it was, for they could see their partner squirm.

Fortunately for Huck, there were other things to be done around the mine than talk. Yet they never lost an opportunity to remind Huck what a fine girl she was. And they meant it, too. Right now Lank Mason had another chance. And, as usual, he didn't let it slip.

"She's a beauty, isn't she?" he said after Sue had left, watching Huck out of the corner of his eye.

The big, tanned puncher was also watching Sue walk past the pumphouse toward the cabin which she shared with Mrs. Donovan.

"Yes," he said, almost to himself, "a beauty."

"I been talkin' to her," said Lank Mason casually. "Been tryin' to persuade her to go home. This mine ain't no place for a girl like her." He wasn't looking at Huck now, but he felt the latter stiffening.

"What did she say?" asked Huck. His voice held little expression.

Purposely Lank withheld his answer for a moment. "She said no," he said. Then he changed the subject. "What are yuh gonna do, Huck, 'bout them yarns of the cuss on El Padre?"

"Keep our ears open," said Huck. "Mebbe we can get our hands on the hombre or hombres spreadin' them damn yarns."

In the weeks that followed Huck was too busy to give the matter further thought. And then one night of wind-thinned moonlight, when the blazing winter stars seemed to brush the ghostly tops of the mountains and frost diamonds sparkled in the silver flood, he heard Lank call him from the inner room of the little cabin they occupied together.

He found the old miner leaning out the open window. Lank motioned to the puncher to join him and listen.

At first Huck could hear nothing but the muted roar of the distant waterfall and the monotonous clank of the pumps that drew the never-ceasing seepage from the lower levels of the mine. Then, filtering through the low rumble and the steady metallic clang, his straining ears caught a muffled throbbing that seemed to come from nowhere and everywhere, rising and falling, rising and falling on the crisply cold air. He glanced questioningly at Lank.

"Injun drums," said the miner. "Injun drums beatin' back in the hills. They're havin' some kind of a tom-tom pow-wow up there. I don't like it."

"I don't suppose it has anything to do with us," Huck demurred. "Tribal dance or feast or something."

"Mebbe," Lank admitted, "but I've heerd them before, and it almost always meant some deviltry was in the wind."

For several minutes they listened to the throbbing of the drums. The moon sank below a crag and weird shadows crept over the cliffs that crouched like monsters waiting to spring and spilled their smoky dust into the canyon depths. Somewhere in the forest that clothed the lower slopes a panther screamed with a desolate unearthly note and an owl hooted solemn answer.

And still the whisper of the drums persisted through the gathering of the dark. The sound appeared to come from the west, with an answering echo from the north. To Huck it suddenly seemed that the drums were "talking," that there was a sinister message sent forth by unseen hands upon the taut heads.

"We will kill you, if we can!" said the hidden men in the west.

"We will kill you, if we can!" said the men in the north.

Each flinging their ominous threat at the gloomy canyon wherein ancient taboos were being broken and long-dead evils brought to light. *"We will kill you, if we can! We will kill you, if we can!"*

Huck went back to bed not quite so skeptical of Old Lank's forebodings. His skepticism vanished altogether when, two days later, the body of a miner who had gone up the cliff top to hunt for grouse and had not returned within a reasonable time was found by a searching party, shot in the back.

Huck immediately gave orders that nobody should wander alone into the hills, particularly along the wooded banks of Dominguez Creek and the old channel, whose frozen pools glittered in the sunlight and were traced by the shadows of the leafless growth which hung over them from either side.

"Stay down here in the canyon where you're safe," he warned his men. "Those red hellions are on the prod for some reason or other and are liable to be snooping around up there in the bush just waiting for a chance to drygulch one of you."

He now renewed his efforts to induce Sue to leave the camp—to go home, or at least to return to Esmeralda until the threat of the evil that hung over the camp like a darkening pall, was lifted.

But she was as determined to stay as he was determined that she go. After a lengthy argument, they finally compromised on Sue's promise to remain close to the camp and cabin at all times. Huck was not entirely satisfied, but he had to be content with the decision.

Moreover, Sue was not his only problem. His mine and his men were his obligation, too.

He was aroused to additional alertness when one night a couple of weeks later the drums throbbed again. Taking no chances, he made a swift check of the camp and was relieved to find all the workers either safe in their cabins or performing duties required of them.

"Reckon they're just making medicine this time, and not celebrating any killings," he told Lank.

XVII

Drums of Death

Two miles south of where Dominguez Creek roared from the mouth of its canyon, the single-track railroad swerved from the creek bank and, for an eighth of a mile or so, after dipping over a crest, followed a gentle down-grade before resuming its steady climb northward at water level. By so doing, it chorded the wide curve made by the creek and saved nearly a mile of distance.

At the foot of the down-grade was a sharp bend around a jutting shoulder of cliff. The long strings of empties, coasting swiftly down the grade, took that curve with screeching wheels and reduced speed before straightening out on the tangent and thundering on toward the canyon mouth.

Five miles below the crest of the rise was a siding upon which empties, and sometimes loads of supplies and machinery, were stored until needed at the mine or until room was made for them in the mine yards inside the canyon. Three miles farther south, the railroad left the gorge of Dominguez Creek below the canyon and bridged the Apishapa River.

From the siding to the bridge, the gorge walls drew together like the narrowing tip of a funnel. Here the tall cliffs overhung the railroad and the hurrying stream which seemed to have thrust aside the walls of eternal rock to reach its destination, the Apishapa. The north abutment of the bridge was at the very tip of the narrowing funnel mouth, with the cliff wall frowning above, the hurrying river washing its submerged base.

Old Mose Baldwell, veteran C. & P. engineer, rumbled a long string of empties, with two cars of dynamite next the caboose, across the bridge, squealed them around the curve where the glowering cliff walls seemed to reach for his engine on either side, and straightened out for the long pull up Dominguez Creek to the mine.

He settled himself comfortably on his seatbox, cocked an eye at his water glass and at the steam gauge, where the needle quivered against the two-hundred-pound pressure mark. He cast an approving glance at his fireman, hauled his reverse lever up a notch and widened his throttle a bit.

The big locomotive responded to his touch

with a faster spinning of her ponderous drivers. Her exhaust cracking, black smoke pouring from her stubby stack, and a squirrel tail of steam drifting back from her trembling safety valve, she roared through the night.

With all that racket of booming stack, grinding wheels and jangling brake rigging, Mose could hardly be expected to hear the low throb of drums far to the north. Even if he had heard them, he would have paid them no heed He would have just worried off another hunk of eatin' tobacco, hauled the cracked peak of his cap a little lower and glinted out the window with his keen eyes. What in time did Injun drums bangin' in the night have to do with railroadin'!

Back in the early days when the C. & P. was pushing its ribbons of steel across the prairie lands and the Sioux and Blackfeet and Crows were disputing every foot of progress, yes, but the Sioux had long since been vanquished, and the mountain Indians had too much respect for the Long Knives, Uncle Sam's blue-clad cavalrymen, to interfere with the railroad. Mail and express robbers were all the railroad man had to worry about now, and Mose and his thundering "556" were hauling neither.

So the "556" snorted beside the winding Dominguez Creek, all too heedless of that ominous throb and mutter in the north, the sound which had sent Huck Brannon scurrying about to

164

check his workers and assure himself none was wandering about the hills.

Old Mose and his fireman were warm and comfortable in their engine cab. The head brakeman dozed on his little perch in front of the fireman's seatbox. The conductor and rear "shack" were equally comfortable in their caboose with the two cars of dynamite swaying along just in front. From his seat in the cupola, the "con" could peer across the tops of the two boxcars and dimly see the long string of empties snaking through the gloom.

Not so comfortable was the lithe young Mexican who shivered in an empty coal car midway along the train. He was not unhappy, however, being of an optimistic turn of mind, and considered momentary discomfort negligible when weighed against the good job he felt confident he would find once he reached the mine.

So he hunched his shoulders against the biting blasts, snugged his sinewy neck down into his turned-up collar and whistled musically beneath his breath. He was unfamiliar with the route over which he was traveling and knew only that his destination was a few miles beyond the lip of the rise over which the big engine would dip in a few minutes.

The "556" topped the rise and rolled down the gentle grade. Old Mose eased his throttle, and, as the last of his train reached the crest, closed it altogether. The long train coasted, Baldwell checking the speed with his engine brake, in preparation for the sharp curve at the foot of the grade. He opened the throttle again as the flanges screeched on the curve and the "556" swung to the change of direction. Around the shoulder of the cliff nosed the big locomotive; and Baldwell slammed his throttle shut again and "dynamited" his train!

Air screeched through the port as he threw on every ounce of pressure in his brake cylinders. All along the train was the clang of brake shoes and the scream of protesting steel. The "556" bucked, reared, rocked like a living thing, then lunged ahead under the shove of the mighty mass of steel ramming her coupler.

With a yell of terror, the fireman went through the window. The head brakeman also "jined the bird gang." Together they rolled down the rocky embankment to lie, bruised and bloody and unconscious, at its foot.

Mose didn't have time to get out. He was still on his seatbox, fighting to save his train, when the "556" crashed into the huge mass of rock that had been levered onto the track. Over she went, thundering and grinding, steam roaring from a torn-off cylinder, her cab smashed, her tender twisted loose from the connecting bar. Gurgling water, snapping coals and hissing air added their quota to the general pandemonium.

There was another sound as Mose Bardwell staggered to his feet, his grizzled head bloody, one arm swinging useless at his side.

It was a sharp, spiteful sound—the crack of a high-power rifle.

Baldwell straightened, an amazed look on his crimson-streaked face. For an instant he stood poised, then he crumpled to the ground and lay motionless.

Lights were bobbing forward from the caboose. The conductor and the rear brakeman, bruised and bleeding, but not seriously injured, were hurrying to the assistance of their less fortunate fellow workers. Heedlessly they ran toward where, very silent, but very sure, death waited. They reached the scene of the wreck, panting for breath, bawling anxious questions. They paused irresolute for an instant, clearly outlined in the glare from the open firebox.

Again the unseen rifle cracked, and again. A moment later, a dozen shadowy forms stole past the bloody bundles that lay beside the still burning lanterns. They picked up the lanterns, cast callous glances at the still forms of the murdered trainmen, and hurried toward the rear of the train.

And from the black shadows inside an empty coal car, dark, burning eyes watched them pass, peered perplexedly at their operations at the rear of the train, and then filled with sudden understanding. On silent feet the young Mexican sped along in the shadow of the motionless cars, past the wrecked engine and on toward the black mouth of Dominguez Canyon.

Huck Brannon instinctively knew it was not time to get up, in spite of the hammering on his door. A glance through the window showed that the winter dawn had not fully broken. And yet old Ah Sing's voice was shrilling to him:

"Get up, Huck! Get up, Huck!"

"What's the matter with you, you yellow hoot-owl?" he bawled in peevish reply. He could hear old Lank cursing inside the inner room, then the solid thump of his bare feet on the floor.

"Get up, Huck!" screeched Ah Sing. "Hell bloke loose!"

Brannon snapped fully awake. He leaped to the door, flung it open. Ah Sing slipped in, beside him a young Mexican who gasped and panted for breath. Despite the bitter cold, his face streamed sweat and his shirt was dark with it.

"Him tell!" barked Ah Sing. "Get dlessed, Huck!"

"They wreck train," panted the Mexican. "I, Pedro, saw all. They work to roll dynamite down the track and so blow up the bridge at the curve."

"Wreck the train where?" Huck asked quietly as he hurried into his clothes.

"At the curve just below canyon mouth," the Mexican replied. "Rocks on track. Shoot engineer —conductor. Dynamite in last two cars."

"Hold it, feller," Huck pointed out. "There's a stretch of north downgrade there. Those cars won't run up hill, and they would have to get over the rise."

"They have the—the—what you call—the move-car."

"Car movers," Huck interpreted.

"*Si, si!* That go click-click on end of pole. They move the cars up the grade little by little. They shove!"

Old Ah Sing screeched weird profanity. Lank, bellowing curses, flung open the door. Huck stopped him with a terse word.

"Wait!" he said. "Don't go off half-cocked. This is going to take some thinking out. It's four miles to that curve. They'll be over the rise 'fore we can get there with men. How many of them are there, Pedro?"

"The dozen, perhaps more," replied the Mexican.

"And all armed," muttered Huck. "Get Smoke," he started to order Ah Sing, then instantly countermanded:

"Nope. No good. Even if I made it, they'd hear me coming and see me. Just wait till I was within rifle range and then pick me off. That wouldn't help a thing.

169

"Lank," the cowpuncher added, "if they get away with this, we're sunk!"

"Hell!" exploded Mason, "that bridge won't take long to put back, even if they do blow it."

"No," Huck replied quietly, "but an explosion at that curve, or anywhere in the gorge for that matter, will bring down the overhanging cliffs and dam the creek—it's sure to. Before anything can be done the water will back up into the canyon and flood our mine. It'll take weeks to pump it out, and cost thousands of dollars we haven't got."

"That damn creek!" growled Mason, glowering through the door at the offending body of water, "it's allus causin' trouble. Was it Injuns wrecked the train, feller?"

"I know not for sure," replied the Mexican. "It was dark and I could not see well. I hear them make talk, and I thought to hear the speech of my people—the Spanish—but I could not be sure because of the rush of the water."

Huck Brannon, tense, motionless, thinking furiously, gave a sudden start.

"Rushing water!" he repeated. "Man, I believe you've hit it!"

Instantly, and heedless of Lank's bewildered sputters, he leaped into action.

The miners were already getting up for breakfast and Huck's bellows brought them boiling from their cabins.

"Crossties!" he ordered. "Half a dozen or so. Get three or four of those heavy stringers and the longest spikes we got. Right over here to the creek bank. Mike, get a car mover and bring it to me."

Within scant minutes he had the railroad ties laid side by side. Men with mauls were spiking them together. The heavy stringers were spiked to them laterally. With miraculous speed a rough, unwieldy, but serviceable, raft was constructed.

"All right, into the water with it," Huck ordered. "Lank, you and the boys break out all the guns we got and hustle down the canyon as fast as you can. Mebbe you'll get there in time to pick off some of those murdering hellions.

"Pedro," he called to the young Mexican, "did you notice whether there were cars on the siding, five miles south of the wreck?"

"*Si,*" the Mexican youth replied. "I see as the train pass. There three—four boxcars."

"Materials for the new tipple," Lank put in. "Not quite ready for 'em and no room to store in the yards."

"Huck! Huck!"

Sue's voice, pregnant with anxiety, suddenly cut the early morning dusk.

Swiftly the men turned toward the running figure. Sue was still drawing on a leather jacket against the morning chill when she reached them. A red flush, apparent even in the dim light, was

171

staining her cheeks to a crimson color. She was out of breath.

"I can't stop now, Sue," cried Huck. He took a step toward her. "But in case something should happen to me—hell!" He swooped down, suddenly had her in his arms, held her for a moment, tight against his breast, kissed her—and then released her.

Sue swayed as she slipped out of his hands.

"Okay," Brannon cried, taking a long pole from the hands of a miner and stepping onto the bobbing raft.

"What you gonna do, Huck?" Lank asked anxiously.

"Stop those hellions from ruining our mine," Huck told him grimly. "All right, you fellers, hand me that car mover, then let go and shove off."

"You'll be kilt!" bawled Lank as the raft swirled into the grip of the current. "You can't outfight a dozen!"

"But maybe I can *out think* 'em," Huck called back as the unwieldy contrivance whisked downstream.

Instantly, however, he had no more time for thinking. The creek ran like a mill race and the rushing water swirled and eddied. Fangs of black rock, with white spray spouting over their ragged edges, broke through the surface and it extended him to the utmost to keep his fragile craft from being capsized or dashed to pieces.

Body rigid, eyes staring, breathing heavily, and standing as though petrified, Sue watched Huck struggling with his raft. The blood had drained from her face and she was now as pale as the ghost light that sifted through the crack of dawn. Suddenly, she came to life.

"Huck!" she cried at the top of her lungs. "Be careful, darling. Be careful!"

But it was doubtful if he heard her, even though she ran along the bank of the river for a space. He was too busy in his fight with the elements. Too busy with eminent danger.

The tough wood of the pole groaned and crackled, bending like a reed as he fought with every atom of his strength to stave off disaster. He whisked through the mouth of the canyon and the dizzy speed, if anything, increased. Far ahead, in the strengthening light, he could see an ominous black pillar rising into the wintry sky—the smoke from the wrecked locomotive. Beyond that would be the grade where the dry-gulchers labored to lift the dynamite cars over the rise.

"Maybe they'll be too busy to notice me pass," Brannon muttered. "If they aren't—"

He grimly left the thought unfinished and devoted all his energies to fighting the raft around a rock-studded bend where the water smoked against glassy walls of stone.

He made it, gasping and panting, sweat beading

his face, the veins of his forehead standing out like cords and black as ink. He straightened his aching back as a stretch of slightly smoother water appeared, and hitched his gun belts a little higher. The creek bank here was clothed by dense growth, but a little farther on the railroad drew nearer to the water and the protecting fringe of growth had been cleared away.

A moment later he saw the shining ribbons of steel writhing up the long and gradual rise. And almost to the crest were the reddish blobs of the two dynamite cars and the caboose. Behind the rear car, crouching figures manipulated the car movers. Others shoved sturdily against the back and sides of the car, which inched slowly upward toward where the ribbons of steel seemed to end and the crest of the ridge stood out hard and clear against the sky.

On shot the raft in the fierce grip of the current, reeling, rocking, swirling through the eddies, grazing deadly fangs of stone. Huck Brannon, cool, alert, eye and muscle perfectly co-ordinated, guided, controlled, averted disaster a score of times. And ahead, the dark line of the railroad drew ever nearer the water's edge and the toiling figures loomed larger and larger.

A shout, thin with distance, sounded above the roar of the water. Huck Brannon cursed bitterly. He was beginning to hope that he might whisk by unnoticed. But that hope was abruptly dashed.

Steadying himself on his precarious perch, he waited.

From the milling group about the dynamite cars mushroomed a puff of bluish smoke. Something wailed through the air close to Huck's head. The cars still moved steadily up the grade, but a number of the pushers had detached themselves from the group and were running toward the creek. The rising sun glinted on the barrels of their rifles.

Another gun cracked, and another slug whined past. Huck measured the distance, planted his feet firmly, took a swift glance downstream. The stretch of water ahead was nearly free from rocks.

The drygulchers raced to the water's edge, shooting as they came. Bullets stormed about the man on the bobbing raft, kicking up fountains of spray, knocking splinters from the ties. One clipped a chip from the pole he held in his hand.

But Huck Brannon waited, alert, gambling his very life against the aim of the running men. Suddenly he dropped the pole and went for his guns.

Out of their sheaths flashed the big Colts as the raft swung toward the bank. The first of the drygulchers was almost to the water's edge.

An instant later he yelled shrilly and plunged into the racing flood. Over his twitching form rolled a crimson ripple; then the current caught the flaccid body and hurled it downstream.

Huck Brannon's long guns gushed reddish flame and wisping spirals of smoke. The reports merged in a drumroll of sound that crackled above the roar of the water and the yells of the drygulchers.

Another man went down, and another. The rest, dodging and ducking, fired wildly with little pretense of aim. A bullet whisked through the sleeve of Chuck's woolen shirt. Another almost slammed his feet from under him as it removed a portion of his boot heel. His hammers clicked on empty shells, he holstered one gun and his hand flew to his cartridge belt.

Then he was past, and before he could reload he was out of pistol range. Rifle bullets whined by, but the raft was reeling and bobbing and the nerves of the killers were shaken. Another instant and a clump of growth hid him from view. On flew the raft, the crest of the rise dwindling and lowering in the distance.

And then over the lip, dark against the sunny sky, the lurching shape of the caboose hove into view. It swayed, dipped, a car followed it, and another. The cargo of destruction moved down the long grade, slowly at first, but gathering speed with every turn of the wheels.

XVIII

Flame and Fury

On raced the raft, the white water lapping over the edges of the timbers, the black fangs of rock racing to meet it, the swirling eddies sucking like hungry mouths. Swiftly it drew away from the rumbling freight cars, until they were but a dim blotch in the distance. A bend and a shoulder of stone hid them from view; but still Huck Brannon could hear that ominous rumble ringing in his ears. His keen glance swept ahead, seeking the siding upon which rested the cars of material destined for the mine—and destined to be its salvation.

From time to time his gaze lifted to the frowning, overhanging cliffs, and each time he shook his head.

"Would be mighty easy if it wasn't for those damn rocks," he muttered. "All we'd have to do is shove the materials cars out on the main line, let the dynamite slam into 'em and blow to glory. But we can't afford to take the chance. Almost as certain to bring down the cliffs here as at the bridge. No, that won't do. If I can just get far enough ahead of those damn runaways!"

177

Anxiously he glanced over his shoulder, back along the shimmering rails that drew together in the distance. Fearfully he expected to see the bulk of the runaways roar around the last curve.

"Not in sight yet, anyway." He breathed relief, and turned to stare ahead.

The raft swept past a clump of growth and Huck saw the materials cars on the siding less than half a mile ahead. Instantly he began to fight the raft toward the outer bank of the stream.

Stubbornly the clumsy craft resisted his muscles, while the current sought powerfully to hurl it back into midstream. For hundreds of yards he didn't seem to gain a foot. Then the raft slowly responded to the pull of his sweating and aching arms. Inch by inch it swerved toward the shore, its speed decreasing as it forged away from the full force of the current.

That slowing added to Huck's anxiety. He could not afford to take too much time in reaching the siding. The runaways would be upon him before he could act. He redoubled his efforts as the head of the siding came opposite him. The strong pole creaked and groaned, bent more and more. He got a purchase on a clump of stone and gave a final mighty shove. The next instant he was sprawling on the spiked crossties, a short section of the shivered pole in his hands. The raft rocked crazily, swung about and headed for midstream once more.

Huck scrambled to his feet, measured the distance to the rocky shore and leaped, the heavy car mover hugged to his breast.

The leap, prodigious though it was, was short. He hit the water with a splash, reeling and swaying. With a surge of thanksgiving he realized he had made it to the shallows. The water was scarcely a foot deep. He kept his footing and scrambled for the bank. Another moment and he was racing toward the materials cars, which stood on the lower end of the siding, but a short distance from the switch stand.

Huck passed the cars and reached the switch stand. A blow of the car mover shattered the lock. He seized the lever and opened the switch. Then he raced back to the cars, scrambled up the ladder of the first one and released the brakes of each in turn. Another instant and he was on the ground, clicking the foot of the car mover beneath a rear wheel of the last car.

The car stubbornly resisted the leverage. Huck rocked his weight on the handle of the mover, surging up and down. There was a groan, a creak, a squeal of protesting metal. The wheel moved a little. Huck frantically worked the lever and the wheel turned more. Then gravity came to his aid and the cars began to slowly move down the siding. Gaining speed, they clattered over the frog and onto the main line.

The cowpuncher swung the switch shut, raced after the moving cars and swarmed up the ladder. As he reached the top a faint, unmistakable rumble came to his ears—the roar of the runaways. Glancing back he saw them, a black blotch swinging around the distant curve.

With appalling speed they rushed toward him. The cars he was riding were also picking up speed, beginning to sway, their wheels clicking out a fast tempo. But as yet it was nothing to that of the rocketing cars of dynamite.

There was nothing Huck could do but wait. He knew he was gambling his life. Already the speed of the car he was riding made leaping to the ground little less than suicide. And if that thundering cargo of destruction caught up with him before the materials cars had gained speed nearly equalling theirs, he would be blown clean to New Mexico by the explosion. Grimly he waited, his hands on the brake wheel of the rearmost car, his narrowed eyes watching the runaways close their distance.

The dope in their journal boxes had caught fire from the terrific friction aroused by the spinning axles. Sheets of flame shot out on either side of the dynamite cars, adding the hazard of fire to that of concussion. Huck shook his head as he watched.

"Even if I get 'em stopped, it'll be a miracle if I get that fire out in time," he muttered. He glanced anxiously ahead, gauging the distance to the deadly curve at the bridge.

The dynamite cars were still closing up, but not so swiftly. Gradually the speed-relation between the two strings became static. Chuck began cautiously to wind up chain on the brake wheel rod. Brake shoes screeched against the wheels; the speed of the materials cars slackened a trifle. And as it slackened, the thundering runaways crept slowly nearer and nearer.

Not quite slowly enough. Huck eased off on the brake wheel a little. The dynamite cars were leaping toward him. His own cars did not respond as readily to the loosened brakes as he had expected. He twirled the brake wheel madly, heard the jangle of the loosened chain, felt the car beneath him hurtle forward to the pull of those in front. Then he was knocked sprawling by the crash of the dynamite cars striking coupler to coupler with the rearmost materials car. Huck held his breath for the explosion—that did not come.

With redoubled speed the lengthened string shot forward. Huck leaped to his feet and frantically twisted the brake wheel until it would turn no more. He raced along the swaying catwalk, leaped across the space separating the reeling cars and twisted another wheel. He had escaped one deadly danger, but another was racing toward him. Already he could see the taller cliffs that marked the narrow gut where Dominguez Creek joined with the hurrying Apishapa, where the rails curved with dizzy sharpness to leap onto the bridge.

He tightened the wheel of the third car to the last notch, turned and sped back the way he had come. He coughed and his eyes stung from the acrid smoke as he leaped onto the foremost dynamite car and spun the brake wheel. Dizzily he reeled back, braked the second car, and then the third. Then he stumbled forward again until he was perched on the foremost materials car, watching the jutting cliffs that marked the curve rush toward him.

Rocking, swaying, lurching, with a screeching of wheels and a mighty squalling of brakes, the string rolled toward the bridge. The flanges of the front wheels hit the curve, and Huck felt them climb. His teeth ground together and his nails bit deep into the flesh of his palms. Then with a clang the wheels fell back upon the rails. He scrambled and clutched as the car swung dizzily around the curve. An instant later it rumbled out onto the bridge, the others, shrieking protest, still following at frightful speed.

Huck breathed deep relief as the string straightened out on the bridge. Then his breath caught in a gasp. Directly ahead a plume of black smoke was rising into the wintry air. Less than a thousand yards distant stood the wreck train, summoned by Lank Mason by telegraph from Esmeralda. There it stood, at what it considered a safe distance from the expected explosion on the far side of the bridge. Toward it roared the runaways, answering to the brakes clamped against the wheels, but still traveling at dangerous speed.

As the dynamite rushed toward it, the wreck train boiled with action. Men leaped from the camp cars and fled madly from the tracks. The plume of black smoke shot upward in a prodigious column streaked with milky swords of steam. Above the rumble of the wheels the roar of the exhaust came to Huck's ears.

The engine's huge drivers spun, grinding flakes of steel and showers of sparks from the rails. They caught, held, spun again. They caught once more, held. Arose a mighty jangle of couplings. The wreck train began to move backward, slowly at first, gathering speed with every turn of the wheels. The exhaust roared and thundered, shooting up clots of fire and clouds of smoke, the siderods clanged, the drivers screeched against the iron. She was moving fast when the runaways hit with a jangling crash.

Again Huck Bannon held his breath as he clung to the reeling catwalk. And once again the impact was not quite severe enough to set off the carefully stored and bolstered dynamite.

The engineer of the wreck train closed his

throttle and began applying his brakes. Before the jostling string had stopped moving, Huck Brannon was down the ladder and on the ground, roaring instructions to the panicky wreckers.

In obedience to his bellowed commands, men came running with buckets of water which they sloshed on the flames eating their way through the sides and bottoms of the cars. The white-faced engineer of the wrecker coupled on a long length of sprinkling hose and together they got the fire under control.

XIX

Turn About

Utterly weary, Huck Brannon sat on a boulder and watched the wreckers beat out the last sparks and prepare to run the dynamite cars back to the siding, so they could proceed to the scene of the wreck.

But Huck was not thinking of the wreck at that moment, nor of his own hairbreadth escapes from death. Moodily he stared straight ahead of him, his black brows drawn together. Finally he arose, stretched his arms above his head and shook himself like a great dog.

"Mountain Indians, hell!" he growled under his breath. "Those hellions that gunned me back there were white men made up to look like Indians—or I'm a sheepherder! The Indians may be in on this shindig, all right, but they're sure not alone!"

Huck rode into town the following day and discovered that Jaggers Dunn had doubled his force of track walkers on the new line and had ordered them armed. He also learned that Cale Coleman had opened a mine twenty miles up the river from Esmeralda.

"Yes, he's got coal," said Jaggers Dunn when Chuck dropped in to talk things over. "It's nothing like stuff you are getting out—not much better than black lignite and with a high sulphur content— but it's marketable in certain sections. His percentage of profit will be small, I figure, because of the distance he will have to ship, but it'll be plenty to pay him to operate. My opinion is that most of the coal which will be developed in this district sooner or later will be more of the type the Coleman mine is working, with perhaps a fair output of good bituminous. Your working is unique to the district, I believe."

"Just as the silver output of the old mine was unique," Huck observed. "Judging from what fragments we found, it was almost pure silver —high grade native metal. Must have been a high old time around that section a few million years ago when all that compression was going on."

"Yes, a flow of molten masses which formed the igneous rocks of the district was responsible, I presume," said Dunn. "No," he replied to a question Huck asked, "no, we won't buy any coal from Coleman—at least not as long as you can supply us; there is no comparison in quality. And, by the way, it wouldn't be a bad idea to step up your production as soon as you are able. I had a little talk with the directors and it has been thought wise to supply the Plains and Western Divisions with Lost Padre coal, if it can be obtained in sufficient quantities."

Huck left the empire builder's office highly elated; and immediately put in an order for supplementary equipment and hired additional hands.

And on the desolate slopes above Dominguez Canyon the drums whispered threateningly and the evil hill gods chuckled in their icy fastnesses upon the mountain tops.

The early morning sun, golden and yellow, was poking its ray-arms over the mountainous ridges and towering purple cliffs that lay like a linked chain around the Apishapa River Valley when Huck and Sue edged their way through the slash the north gap made on entering the valley.

They reined in and stood their horses, silent

before the mighty spectacle of the sunrise breaking over the huge, almost oval valley. Beneath them, sinuous and slithering, ran the silver-streaked Apishapa River. Their eyes followed its winding course until it slipped through a gorge at the far end of the valley, and disappeared from sight.

"It's lovely here, Huck," said Sue, lips parted, eycs glistening.

"It's mighty fine," Huck agreed. "I sure—" He opened his mouth to say something further; but hesitated and decided against it.

"What is it, Huck?"

"Nothing," he replicd, feeling her eyes on his face. "I was just going to say again how pretty this valley is," he added lamely.

"What a cattleman couldn't do with this spread," said Sue, almost to herself. But the words rang in Huck's ears.

"Yes," muttered Huck under his breath. "I sure could."

"What?"

"Huh?" ejaculated Huck, afraid that Sue had heard him. "Nothing. Talking to myself."

She laughed. "Don't let anyone hear you, Huck," she said. "They might think you escaped from an asylum."

"Maybe they'd be right," Huck muttered to himself. Then aloud: "I've got a lot of things on my mind."

187

He felt her eyes on him again, but avoided looking at her. Since that day at the river bank when he had yielded to a mad impulse—the same impulse called forth by seeing her that day when she first arrived in Esmeralda—he had avoided not only looking at her, but being alone with her.

He cursed himself again, now, for having suggested to her this morning that they ride out to the Apishapa River Valley. He hardly knew then why he had made the suggestion. But now it was clear to him. Perfectly clear.

He wanted her to see—and approve—the spread that he one day would own. Yes, he told himself, he would one day own it—and maybe in the not-too-distant future. The minute he had laid eyes on it when he first came there, he knew that this was what he had been looking for. This was the spread he'd been seeking. This valley held the object of his search.

Through the corner of his eyes he stole a look at her. But she seemed far from guessing at his secret. Slim and erect, she was sitting her horse, her eyes focused on the valley bed. Her cheeks were flushed and her eyes held a deep and inward gleam. He was reminded of the day they rode the herd up to Stevens Gulch to shove them aboard the train headed for Kansas City. The day that he had said good-bye to her—without knowing it, of course.

She had the same look on her face then; the same look of shyness, mixed with eagerness. Suddenly she turned to him.

"I'm glad you brought me here, Huck," she said. "It's beautiful. I oughtn't say it—but it's as good to look at as the Bar X spread. Maybe even better."

"That's hard on the Bar X, Sue," said Huck, glad to get off the subject. "I reckon your father wouldn't be pleased to hear you say that."

"I don't know," she replied seriously. "I think even Dad would agree with me."

"Not Doyle," cried Huck. "For him the Bar X spread is the most beautiful thing this side of heaven—and I calculate I'd think the same if I stood in his boots."

"But what do you think of the Apishapa Valley, Huck?" asked Sue softly.

Her head was turned so he couldn't see what she was driving at—if anything.

"I figure," he said casually, "it's the likeliest looking spread my eyes have set on in a year of Sundays."

"I wouldn't be surprised," she said, still without turning her head, "to hear one day that some smart business man bought up this valley, and stocked it with cattle. They would grow big and fat here. They've got water, plenty of good grass, likely looking spots to winter in—why, the valley has everything."

A darting pang of fear knifed through Huck at the possibility voiced by Sue—that someone would take this spread away from him before he could claim it. He grew angry as he realized she was right—and knew that he couldn't do anything about it, for the time being at least. There were other obligations to be met first. Maybe in a few months or so. He shrugged his shoulders to drive away presentiments. Yet the fear had taken root and began to grow.

"Yes," he admitted. "This valley's got everything."

"It would be a pity," continued Sue, softly yet relentlessly, "if the wrong party got hold of it. Cale Coleman, for instance."

He almost growled as he turned swiftly toward her. Yet she seemed innocent of any guile as she gazed fixedly on some far point down below, alongside the Apishapa River that chased a stream of silver through the valley.

Lank Mason had told him that about a month past, during a visit made by him and Sue to Esmeralda to pick up some supplies and provender for the kitchen, they had encountered Coleman. The latter had gazed with undisguised admiration at Sue, although he said nothing to either of them.

In the interim, Sue had learned something of Coleman's character and needed no persuasion to stay away from the richest man in

Esmeralda, for she had taken an instinctive dislike to him.

Suddenly Huck smiled. She was smart, all right. But he could see through her game. She was trying to get a rise out of him. However, two could play at that game. So when he spoke, it was with an easy air of nonchalance.

"Yes," he said. "You're dead right. It sure would be a pity if an hombre like Coleman got hold of this valley."

Now she turned to gaze at him. But her expression was unfathomable.

"If I remember correctly," she said, "I think I knew a cowboy once who would be mighty interested in this spread."

"Who?"

"Someone who used to work for my dad," she replied. "Can't seem to recollect his name, but he was awfully anxious to own a piece of his own land—to stock it, and raise—"

"Yes," Huck interrupted her. "I know who you mean. I know the man. Only he got mixed into the mining business and kind of forgot all about being a cowboy. He got so busy, I reckon he forgot about everything else, too."

He saw Sue turn her face quickly to one side as though she had been attracted by the flight of a bird, or the echo of rock falling down the mountainside. He wasn't sure, but he thought he saw a shadow pass over her face. Perhaps it was only a cloud that momentarily hid the sun from the earth.

"I think we ought to start back to camp," Sue said. "Mrs. Donovan is going to need me."

"Okay," agreed Huck. "Let's go."

Slowly they turned their horses, almost with reluctance it seemed, and headed back through the north gap. Not once, however, did either turn back to look at the Apishapa River Valley.

XX

Spring Rains

Spring arrived, and brought with it the drenching rains of Spring. Dominguez Canyon was choked with swirling mist through which the level lances of water drove with icy force. Tight gray buds were swelling and bursting on bush and shrub, the pines were a fresher green and emerald tendrils reached like questing witch fingers from the brown stalks of the vines.

Dominguez Creek, a rushing brown flood, boomed down the side wall of the canyon and hurried to join the bustling Apishapa. The streaming black sides of a string of loaded coal cars on the siding near the mine mouth glistened wetly in the flicker of light from the gaunt buildings that housed the pumps, boiler and winding engine.

The cabins of the miners were dark; for tired men were taking well earned rest. Suddenly, however, light flickered in one set on the bank of the old creek bed and at no great distance from the railroad tracks.

"Huck," a voice called inside the cabin, "them hellions is at it again!"

Huck Brannon glanced at his watch, saw it was little more than an hour before time to get up, and slipped on his clothes before joining Lank Mason at the window. Leaning out beside the miner, the cool drops of the rain bathing his face, he listened to the throb and mutter of the unseen drums.

"Lively t'night," Lank grunted. "Sound clost, too."

Suddenly the mutter ceased, then broke forth again in a staccato roll from the north. A deep-toned mutter answered in the west, then silence broken only by the swish of the rain, the muffled pound of angry water and the monotonous clank of the pumps.

"What's that?" exclaimed Lank, leaning far out the window.

"Sounded like an explosion of some kind," said Huck, straining his ears to listen, "and what's *that?*"

Above the clanking of the pumps sounded a rolling mutter that steadily grew in volume—a hissing, rushing mutter that was almost instantly a rising roar.

"Water!" exclaimed Huck. "Lot's of it! Coming fast! What the—"

His voice was suddenly drowned by a booming thunder and a tremendous liquid crashing. Over the end wall of the canyon boiled a frothing flood that cascaded down the face of the cliff, wiped out the mouth of the mine and smashed and scattered equipment. Huck saw the lights of the winding engine house blotted out as by a giant hand.

With a prodigious crackling the flimsy little building went to pieces that were tossed away on the flood that rolled down the old bed of Dominguez Creek. Water was frothing around the cabin, gushing over the sill. The yells of the terrified miners sounded through the tumult. Half-clad men poured from the cabins, shouting profane questions in many languages.

"Cloudburst!" howled Lank Mason. "Cloudburst back in the hills!"

"Cloudburst, hell!" Brannon roared. "Get some clothes on. Get outa here! We've got to save the pumphouse! The water's rising around it and it'll go like the winding engine house in another minute! If those pumps are smashed the lower levels will fill up and it'll take weeks to pump

194

'em out again! C'mon before we're sunk!"

Grabbing a lantern and lighting it, he rushed from the cabin. An instant later he was roaring directions to the bewildered miners.

Under the dynamic driving force of the cowboy's personality, order quickly replaced chaos. The miners, reassured by the confidence in his voice, responded quickly. Lank Mason's half-dozen hard-rock men remembered that they were trusted foremen and stock owners in the mine and began functioning with their customary efficiency.

"Grab car movers and get those cars of coal down here opposite the pumphouse," Huck told them. "Knock open the dump doors and let the coal run out. Bank it between the cars and up against their sides. That'll shut off the water from the pump house. Buttress the coal with rocks and beams."

Sue appeared with Mrs. Donovan close behind her. Huck took one look at them and roared.

"Sue, Mrs. Donovan—head for higher ground. Ah Sing, go with them. No telling when hell is going to break loose around here."

Without another word, he turned toward his men. There was nothing left for the three to do but to follow Huck's orders.

Cursing, the Mexican miners swarmed to work.

Although there was water on the floor of the pumphouse and hissing on the hot ashes beneath the boiler, the monotonous clanking of the pumps still went on. The engineer, shaker bar in hand, stood ready to dump his fires if necessary and avoid clinkering his grates. Dubiously he watched the water level rise, then cursed profound relief as it remained stationery and began to recede.

"You got it, Boss!" he bellowed to Huck Brannon. "She's goin' down! You got it beat! But how in the blankety-blank-blank we gonna get inter the mine 'thout divin' suits?"

Water was still roaring down the cliff wall in unabated volume. Huck stared at the yellow torrent, and then turned to his grouped men.

"Get sledges and drills and picks and blasting powder," he told them. "Lank, you and the foremen bring rifles. Sift sand, now, before the whole yard is washed away. The crick is rising by the minute and we'll have an unholy flood on our hands to add to our troubles if we don't straighten out this mess pronto."

Down the canyon, sloshing through pools, stumbling over partially submerged boulders, he led his laden crew. Lank Mason and the six foremen, Winchesters tucked under arms, followed close behind the cowboy in grim silence. They were beginning to understand what had happened and were seething with anger.

Leaving the canyon, they clambered into the streaming hills and turned sharply north. The gray dawn of a rainy morning had fully broken when they reached the juncture of the natural bed of Dominguez Creek and the old man-made channel.

"See how they did it?" Huck remarked to Lank.

He pointed upstream past where he and his partners had turned the creek back into its natural bed, months before.

Lank stared, cursing bitterly. "Did jest 'bout the same as that damned old Spaniard did nigh onto a hundred years back," he growled. "They dug the old channel a little further upstream, turnin' it to the west, walled it up good and high where it paralleled the cut we made, and then blowed what was left of the crick bank up 'bove here.

"Course the water turned inter the channel which was again jest a little lower than the upper crick bed. Worked in that big thicket up ahaid, where nobody'd see them and picked a nice rainy night to finish the job. No wonder they was poundin' their damn drums last night—crowin' over whut they'd done to us! But how in blazes did they do all this work 'thout anybody seein' 'em?"

"Remember nobody has been coming up here since Montez was murdered last winter," Huck pointed out. "Begins to look like they figured that a killing would stop everybody from coming up here. We played right into their hands. C'mon and let's get up where they made the cut. We've got to turn this water back where it belongs and then rip this channel to pieces so's they can't pull this stunt again."

The rain had stopped and the sun was shining brightly through chinks in the thinning clouds. It was the brilliant sunshine, and Huck Brannon's keen eyesight and uncanny gift for noticing anything out of the ordinary, that saved the party.

It was only a quick glint flashing from the dense thicket ahead, but it was enough.

"Down! Down behind the rocks!" the cowboy yelled.

Without an instant's hesitation his followers obeyed, falling flat on their faces the instant before puffs of smoke spurted from the undergrowth and lead stormed through the air.

Almost before the crackle of the reports had ceased, Huck was on his feet again, zigzagging for the thicket, ducking, weaving, slewing from side to side, both guns out and blazing. Behind him Lank and his men hammered the thicket with rifle bullets.

From the growth sounded yells of pain and anger. This was more than the drygulchers had counted on. They had doubtless been licking their lips over the helpless victims who would walk blindly into their trap. An entirely different matter were those blazing sixguns and roaring rifles. As Huck and his posse swooped down on the thicket, the brush was smashing and crackling with the passage of running forms. They crashed into the growth just in time to hear the clatter of swift hoofs speeding into the north.

"Had horses all ready to trail rope," panted the cowboy. "Hold it—it's no use running our legs off for nothing."

"Here's a couple what ain't goin' anywhere!" Lank called grimly. "Damn their red hides!"

Huck stared down at the two dead men. One was undoubtedly a full-blooded Goshoot Indian. The other he was inclined to believe was a half-breed, but he could not be sure. Both were dressed in dirty buckskins and boot moccasins.

"Damn good guns for Injuns to carry," growled Lank, picking up a well oiled repeater.

"This feller's sportin' a brand new Smith and Wesson, too," said one of the foremen, pulling the big six from its holster.

Huck went through the dead men's pockets, turning out a miscellany of junk to which he attached no particular significance. A cunningly concealed pouch under the half-breed's belt yielded something of interest—two bright and shiny ten-dollar gold pieces.

"Brand new!" the cowboy muttered, turning them over in his slim fingers. "Look like they just come out of a bank—haven't been carried hardly at all."

The concentration furrow was deep between his black brows as he stared at the gold. He glanced again at the expensive guns with which the Indians had been armed.

"Looks like the hellions made a mighty good raid plumb recent," remarked Lank Mason, "one what paid them plenty."

"Yes," agreed Brannon, staring into the south with somber eyes, "one that paid them plenty."

XXI

Blood and Steam

It took a full day of hard work to get Dominguez Creek back where it belonged, and a good deal more than a week to repair the damage done to the mine equipment.

During that week, the C. & P. firemen of the Mountain Division cursed fervently as they wrestled with clinkered grates and clogged flues, the result of the low-grade coal the road had to accept from the Cale Coleman mine.

The coal wasn't good, but the saving over what it cost to transport fuel from distant points was too great to be ignored. The road bought from Coleman while the Lost Padre was shut down and Cale pocketed a nice profit.

"It's a ill wind what don't blow nobody no

good," misquoted Old Tom Gaylord, "but why the hell did it hafta blow good to that hyderphobia skunk? Blankety-blank-blank them Injuns, anyhow!"

The Lost Padre got back into operation, the C. & P. firemen sighed prodigious relief, and for a while the drums muttered no more from the northern hills.

"Cal'late we sorta give 'em their come-uppance when we blasted a coupla them loose from their greasy hides," said Lank Mason. " 'Sides, the way we cut and walled that channel, there ain't no chance for 'em to raise any more hell up there, and the way the railroad is patrolled 'tween here and town, that section's pretty safe. Looks like we may have easy goin' from now on."

Huck Brannon hoped the miner was right, but was not entirely optimistic. Those two shiny gold pieces still puzzled Huck.

"And what's a feller that looks like an Apache 'breed doing with the mountain Goshoots?" he asked Old Tom. "And that job on the crick was done almighty smooth for an ignorant Indian outfit."

"You figger mebbe somebody 'sides the Injuns had somethin' to do with it?" Old Tom asked. "Who could it be?"

However, Huck did not care to hazard an answer to that question—yet.

There came a day of *fiesta* in the Mexican

quarter in Esmeralda. It also happened to be payday at the Lost Padre mine, and a Saturday. So Huck gave his Mexican pitmen the weekend off so they could properly celebrate the feast.

Lank and the foremen decided to go to town also and see the fun. Old Ah Sing was in town purchasing kitchen supplies.

And Mrs. Donovan had invited Sue to spend the day with her in town. The mere thought of missing a *fiesta* made Mrs. Donovan shudder. And the picture of the colorful celebration painted by her friend appealed to Sue, so that she too was eager to go.

Which left Huck and the night engineer at the pump house in full charge of the mine. Huck had even dispensed with the two night watchmen, taking over their duties himself so that they would have the chance to enjoy themselves with their friends.

"The boys all work hard and never complain," he told the red-headed engineer as the grinning and cheering crew waved good-bye from the empty coal car which was taking them to town. "They deserve to have a little fun now and then."

"The saddle-colored hellions are good fellers when you get to know 'em," the engineer agreed, cutting off a chunk of amazingly strong and black tobacco from a plug and stuffing it into an equally amazingly strong and blackened pipe. "When I had that bad sick spell last month, two of 'em insisted on settin' up all night with me, after having worked hard all that day and having to work hard the next. Treat 'em right and they treat you right, and glad of the chanct."

The day wore on without event and the lovely blue dusk sifted down from the flame-wrapped mountain tops to brim the canyon with purple shadows. Stars like points of golden fire pierced the black velvet of the sky and a soft little wind chuckled around in the tree tops and wondered where to go next.

It was a silent night, with only the low rumble of Dominguez Creek and the steady clank of the pumps to break the hush. Huck Brannon, smoking outside his cabin, his chair propped back against the wall and the high heels of his boots hooked over a rung, was filled with a quiet content. Dreamily he watched the great clock in the sky wheel from east to west.

In his musing, the clock took the shape of a face. A familiar face. The corners of his gray eyes crinkled in the slow beginnings of a smile. To an observer, it might have looked as though Huck Brannon were settling back in his chair prepared to enjoy himself in pleasant recollections.

Thought of Sue Doyle gave him a curious sense of well-being, and of optimism. Barring accidents in the mine, he would soon be in a position to speak his piece to her. To tell her how soft he had gone over her. To tell her that he had not meant what he said that day they rode into the Apishapa River Valley. That he really wanted that spread more than he wanted anything else in the world—with one exception, of course. And that he had set his heart on it long ago, and always thought of it as his.

Yes, he would soon be in a position to pay Old Man Doyle back the five thousand dollars he had borrowed from him—and then borrow, permanently, the Old Man's daughter. Fair exchange, he thought, grinning. No, it was not. He, Huck, was getting the better of it— by a long, long shot.

A sense of well-being and contentment enveloped Huck Brannon.

He could see the intermittent glow of the engineer's pipe where he took his seat beside the pump-house door. Otherwise there was no sign of life in the valley. Even the owls were silent and the panthers had evidently enjoyed good hunting and were too well filled to do any squalling.

Suddenly, however, sounds of life broke the silence. Somebody was coming up the canyon, and coming fast. Huck could hear the clatter of hoofs and a prodigious blowing. His booted feet dropped to the ground and he stood up, peering through the darkness.

"What the hell?" called the engineer, who was also standing.

A shadow flickered through the bar of light streaming through the open door of the pump house and slithered to a halt. In another instant old Ah Sing flung himself from the back of his mule and came pattering across to Huck's cabin.

"What the hell's wrong with *you?*" demanded the puncher.

The Chinaman's face was working convulsively, his beady eyes snapping with excitement. He was blowing almost as hard as the sweat streaked mule.

"Men come!" he gurgled. "Injun men!" He gulped, sputtered and relapsed into crackling Chinese that sounded like shot rolling around in a tin can.

"Stop it!" barked Brannon. "Shut up and get your breath and then talk sense! What about Indian men?"

"Come to bust mine," said Ah Sing, gaining some degree of calmness. "Be soon come damn quick. Got guns—sledge hammels—heap damn mad!"

"Start at the beginning," Huck told him tersely. "How'd you find this out?"

"Me lidin' to mouth of canyon," replied Ah Sing. "Almost to—see light up 'longside cliff west of canyon mouth. Think funny—go see. Men sit 'lound camp fi', eat, talk—talk Spanish talk—me know Spanish talk, listen. Talk othel talk, too—me no know—Injun talk. They wait till moon go topside 'neath, then come—bust mine. Me tie bullos with glub in thicket—come fast on mule. Can do!"

"How many were there?" Huck asked quietly, hitching his double cartridge belts a little higher.

"Mebbe twenty-fi' and half," replied Ah Sing.

"Thirty-five or forty eh?" Huck translated. "You sure they Indian men, Ah Sing?"

"Most. Some Injun-half, mebbe Mexican-half, not many."

For a moment Huck stood staring down the dark canyon. Ah Sing waited expectantly. Mike, the engineer, muttered vivid profanity and picked up a heavy spanner.

"Come to bust mine," Huck repeated Ah Sing's words. "That means to smash the pumps and the winding engine. Smash the pumps and it'll take weeks to install new ones. And then more weeks to pump out the lower levels. Which will mean the finish of the Lost Padre, so far as we are concerned. Stop the pumps for any length of time and she'll fill up to the top of the shaft. Always been a wet mine—wetter'n ever since they sent the crick down the channel."

XXII

Pain and Panic

He frowned as he recalled Lank's report of a much greater volume of water coming from the cave in which the murdered Indians slept, the flow of which had been gradually lessening since the opening of the mine. The seepage in the lower levels had also greatly increased and the pumps were hard put to keep the workings free of water.

His slim hands dropped to the butts of the heavy sixes swinging low on either thigh, and his face grew grim as he eyed the silvery half-disc of the moon still peering over the lip of the western wall. Soon that moon would be behind the western crags—"top-side 'neath," as Ah Sing had expressed it.

Then the group would creep silently up the gloom filled canyon, knowing that only two men had been left there by the departing celebrants, and hoping for a quick surprise and little or no resistance.

"They're the ones due for a surprise, though!" the cowboy growled, tightening his grip on his guns. There were rifles in the cabin, and Ah Sing and the engineer could shoot after a fashion.

Still, the odds were heavy. And there was something else that caused Huck Brannon to hesitate. From Ah Sing's report, it appeared that the majority of the raiders were actually mountain Indians—people who really believed that the reopening of *La Mina del Padre* was fraught with evil for them. Leaning their belief as they did on the traditions that had come down to them, heaven knew they had cause to think so, Huck was forced to admit.

They might be led by men who had other and more selfish interests in mind, men who had fanned the embers of superstition into flame to further their own ends, but the Indians were doubtless sincere enough in their beliefs. And Huck Brannon had a decided aversion to shooting down men who were doing what they believed to be right and acting under honest motives, no matter how mistaken they might be.

Huck Brannon, unlike many cattlemen, believed that Mexicans, Indians and other "lesser tribes without the law" had their rights to be respected, and had in them the making of good citizens if given the chance.

He did not propose to have his property destroyed by predatory interests, but he was determined that misguided dupes were not going to die at his hand if he could possibly prevent it.

He racked his brains as he stared down the valley for some means of stopping the raiders without actually destroying them.

It was the sudden sputtering hiss of the safety valve on the big boiler which furnished steam to operate pumps and winding engine that gave him inspiration.

The engineer automatically stepped into the pump-house and opened the injector, which sent a stream of cold water into the over-pressured boiler. He glanced at rising water gauge and falling steam needle and shut the injector. He turned and bumped into Huck Brannon, who was striding into the pump house.

"Hey!" bawled Mike in an injured tone, stumbling back and rubbing his bruised nose.

Huck paid no attention to his protest.

"I've got it, Mike!" he exclaimed. "I know how we can stop them without killing them! It's a cinch."

"Huh?" grunted Mike, staring.

Ah Sing, pattering at Huck's heels, crowed exultantly.

"Can do! Me betcha you me!" he declared.

"Quick!" exclaimed Huck, "screw a sleeve into the blow-off cock at the base of the boiler—a sleeve with a union on the other end. Use a reducing bushing if you have to, and attach that big leather hose to the sleeve. Hurry, you grease monkey—you may have to cut threads on the sleeve, and we haven't got all night—moon's almost down!"

Grunting profane admiration, the little engineer went to work, swiftly and efficiently. Huck and Ah Sing meanwhile extinguished the lights in Huck's cabin and banked the front wall of the pump house with coal and timbers to stop the passage of bullets through the flimsy planks.

"I got yore damn hose pipe fastened onto the cock," Mike called before they had finished their task. "Moon's outa sight," he added heavily.

Huck nodded and extinguished all the lights except one carefully shaded lantern. He examined the length of hose closely. It was new and strong and capable of taking plenty of pressure.

"Open the blow-off cock about half way when I give the word," he told Mike. "Don't open it all the way till we open the nozzle cock. If this damn thing bursts with that blow-off open, we'll all three be parboiled like a salt-bacon rind. All right, now, take it easy and listen. I don't want 'em to get too close."

The last faint glimmer of the moonlight faded above the western canyon wall. Darkness, intense and silent, filled the gorge. The mutter of the falls and the clank of the pumps sounded unnaturally loud to the straining ears.

An owl hooted sadly and the sudden blood-chilling scream of a panther punctuated his lonely plaint. Mike swore under his breath and Ah Sing muttered something in Cantonese that was certainly not a prayer.

Huck Brannon, peering through the narrow window, said nothing, and it was Huck's keen ears that caught the first faint scrape of a moccasined foot on a loosened stone.

There was a considerable open space fronting the pumphouse, and in this space the stars threw a faint, elusive glimmer. Not much, but enough to etch the dark clump shadow that moved cautiously out of the growth, hesitated for an instant and then drifted forward in utter silence.

In that tingling silence, Huck Brannon's ringing voice was like the explosion of a shell.

"*Alto!* Halt!" he thundered in clear Spanish. "Don't come a step closer. We're ready for you and can put you down before you're halfway to the doors! Get the hell out of this canyon while you're in one piece," he added in English.

The stealthy shadows froze as if turned to stone. Guttural exclamations sounded. For a moment it seemed as if the surprise-numbed raiders were going to rush from the gorge. Then a voice rang out, peremptory, commanding, vicious in intonation:

"It ees lie! There ees but two men there! Forward!"

The English words were followed by ripping guttural syllables that Huck could not understand. Screeching yells answered, and a spatter of shots.

A bullet or two whined through the open window, but Huck was standing well to one side, Mike cursed as one caromed off the boiler face and spattered him with splinters of lead. Outside sounded a rush of padding feet.

Huck Brannon gripped the hose nozzle in gloved hands and stepped close to the window.

"All right, Mike," he said quietly.

The engineer's wrench rasped against the blow-off cock. The hose writhed like a snake as the scalding water pounded into it. Huck felt the strong leather pipe swell to the bursting point.

The yelling, shooting crowd had crossed half the distance of the open space when Huck Brannon, risking a chance bullet, stepped to the window and thrust the glistening brass nozzle through the opening. Eyes narrowed to slits and smokily green, his face set in lines bleak as chiseled granite, he turned the nozzle cock.

Driven by the terrific power of the internal steam, the scalding water shot from the nozzle with a wicked hiss. Huck twitched the tip of the nozzle in a short horizontal arc, elevating it slightly.

Beyond the cloud of steam that roared up in front of the window, the screeching warwhoops changed to shrieks and screams of agony. Huck stood well forward now, having no further fear of bullets. He elevated the nozzle still more and drenched with the scalding spray the packed men behind the front rank of the raiders. He devoutly hoped that the instigators of the attack had been in the van and had borne the brunt of that first driving burst of boiling water.

Louder and wilder came the yells. There was a sound of hectic scrambling over the loose boulders, then the rattling thud of racing feet that had lost all interest in maintaining any sort of silence. Huck swished the nozzle, raising it as much as he dared. Fresh howls arose, swiftly receding from the vicinity of the pumphouse.

"Off, Mike, off!" Huck shouted.

As he heard the engineer's wrench clang against the blowoff, he snapped the nozzle cock shut, dropped the hose and slid both big guns from their holsters. Aiming high, he pulled triggers as fast as his thumbs could fan the hammers back. Taking his cue from the rattling crash of the reports, old Ah Sing fired through the roof with a Winchester until he had emptied the magazine.

Far down the gorge yells of pain and panic still echoed, but soon they became only a drone in the distance and then died away altogether.

Brannon grunted as he reloaded and holstered his guns. "I kept the nozzle up pretty well," he told the engineer. "I don't figure I more than scorched 'em good and plenty."

"You'd had oughta give 'em the full force," growled Mike. "If they'd got in here, there wouldn't have been enough left of any of us to grease a saw blade. You figger they're all gone and ain't comin' back?"

Huck thought so, but to make sure, Ah Sing with a knife held between his toothless gums, slipped out like a yellow snake to reconnoiter. Twenty minutes later he came puffing back, his arms full of hardware.

"Plenty good lifles and sledge hammels left," he chuckled creakily, thudding several new Winchesters to the floor. "Injun man no can find. Lun plenty damn fast. Laundly wolk pick up in Injun town, me betcha you me!"

Chuck cautioned Ah Sing and Mike to say nothing about the affray. He stored the hammers and guns dropped by the raiders in their flight; and when the pitmen came back to work there was nothing to indicate the hectic event that had taken place in their absence. One of the foremen, however, gave out a bit of interesting information.

"Musta had one helluva time over in the Mexican quarter," the foreman, who had spent most of his time in the Blue Whistler saloon bucking the tiger, told Huck. "This mawnin' jest 'fore we piled inter the car to come back to camp, I saw three, four jiggers all tied up like pigs in pokes. One was that blackfaced Estaban Garcia what does odd jobs for Jeff Eades, the drift foreman at the Coleman gold diggin's. Couldn't see hardly anythin' of him but his eyes.

I asked him what the hell happened and he spit out a string of Spanish I couldn't make head or tail of and the way he looked murder at me outa them pig eyes, I thought he's gonna stick a knife in me. You'd think, from the way he looked, that I'd had something to do with him bein' wrapped up in rags thataway!"

XXIII

Blazing Doom

In his office not far from the mouth of the mine, Huck Brannon glanced approvingly at a balance sheet and bank statement lying before him on his desk.

Outside, the mellow sunshine of late Autumn streamed over the western lip of the canyon wall. The shadows were long across the canyon floor and a few minutes later the pumphouse whistle tooted a shrill blast. The workers on the loading tipple came clattering down the stairs, laughing and joking among themselves, and soon clots of men, the black smudges of their toil upon their faces, trickled from the mine mouth.

Huck could hear the whine of the winding engine raising the cages from the lower levels.

Soon the workers of the upper levels would leave the mine, it being a rule that the lower levels should always be emptied first for safety's sake. The ratchet of the big drum clicked for the last time and the sinuous cable came to a halt. The lower levels were cleared of men.

Huck glanced up as Lank Mason entered. He nodded to his partner and held up the balance sheet.

"Well, we're even up now and a little better," he told the big miner. "Looks like we're due to make a little *dinero,* after all, feller."

"Yep, even if old Don Fernando de Castro did send all the silver to Spain or carted it off to Hell with him," chuckled Lank. "We don't need his darned silver!"

Lank walked to the inner room to wash up. Huck turned back to his figures.

And then—the window glass smashed to fragments, the chairs danced on their legs, the whole building rocked and swayed like in a hurricane. The air quivered to a pulsing roar which was followed by a terrible silence broken only by the monotonous clank of the pumps.

Dazed, numbed, Huck Brannon picked himself up from the floor, to which he had been flung as by a giant hand. Outside was a pandemonium of yelling voices. Lank Mason, swabbing at his bloody face, came pounding from the inner room.

"It's a blow!" he yelled.

Huck darted to the door. Black smoke was pouring from the mine mouth. Men were running madly about, shouting insanely. Huck saw one of the lower drift foremen hurrying toward the mine.

"Is everybody out, Watt?" he roared to the man.

"Lower levels," the foreman shouted back. "Forty or fifty men still in the upper."

Huck darted to the pump house. Mike, the engineer, was pulling levers, testing, examining, staring at the falling hand of the pressure gauge.

"Blower system's gone to hell," he barked in answer to Huck's question. "Winding engine can't move the cage to the lower levels. Pumps is still suckin' water."

Huck ran outside again. The mine no longer vomited smoke in dense clouds, but wreaths and whorls still floated up the cliff face. Men were reeling through the smoke, now, burned, bruised, bloody. Huck and Lank and the foreman checked them as they emerged. Their faces grew stern as the blackened trickle dwindled and ceased.

"Twenty-two short," said Brannon quietly after a wait of long minutes during which the mine mouth yawned emptily save for vagrant wisps of smoke that continued to drift forth.

Huck eyed those recurrent wisps with a darkening face. There was an ominous threat in them. They might be but the residue of pockets that remained in the rooms after the blowers ceased to function.

But they might mean that the explosion of methane gas had set fire to the mine. In which case, other explosions might follow, especially as the blower system which tended to lessen the accumulation of gas had broken down.

After a wait of several more minutes, Huck turned to the foremen and miners clustered about the tunnel mouth.

"All right," he said quietly. "Volunteers. Who'll go with me to look for those twenty-two men and bring them out, if any of them are alive? Wait," he said as Lank and the three foremen stepped forward. He pointed to the drifting smoke wreaths. "You all know what that means," he said significantly. "Don't forget the chance you're taking. Nobody *has* to go."

"Hell!" grunted old Lank in reply.

The foremen snorted derisively. Men began to crowd forward.

"All right," said Huck, and his voice was a trifle unsteady, "but you can't all go. So we'll take only single men. Single men to the front, six will be enough."

Half a dozen brawny young miners shouldered up ahead of the others.

"Back, Miguel," growled one, giving a companion a shove that sent him sprawling. "You have the old mother and the two young sisters."

"And you—Pedro—you are betrothed to three in *Mejico* and the saints alone know how many more elsewhere!" the indignant Miguel bawled. "Would you widow a village?"

"What terror, think you, holds Senor Death for me, *amigo?*" replied Pedro with a flash of white teeth.

Quickly Huck picked his crew from the eager volunteers. Scant minutes later, equipped with tools, blasting powder and restoratives, the body of men marched into the mine.

Most of the smoke appeared to have escaped, but the gas content of the atmosphere was dangerously high, as proved by the increasing glow of the gauze envelopes of the safety lamps.

"If we don't run into choke-damp, we'll be lucky," muttered Brannon.

He knew that even more dreaded and deadly was the heavy, low-lying "damp," mainly carbon dioxide, that all too often choked to death the survivors of the explosion of fire damp, the miners' term for methane.

"Wait," cried Huck suddenly. He held up a hand in warning, and listened intently. He turned on his heel.

A cry, long and drawn out, had come, seemingly from the direction in which they had just come—the entrance to the mine. Then they all heard, in the distance, the sound of running feet approaching them.

"Wonder who it is?" snapped Lank Mason, his nerves on edge.

"We'll see in a minute," said Huck. "Whoever it is, is coming in a hurry. Must be plenty important."

A figure emerged from a bend in the tunnel, and as the flickering light from the safety lamps picked out the features, a gasp ran through the men.

"Sue!" thundered Huck, astounded and angry at the same time. "What in blazes are you doing here?"

She stopped to catch her breath, and she stood speechless for a moment, facing them, brushing back from her eyes her raven-black hair which had become disheveled in her pursuit of the men. Her face seemed ruddy in the lamplights, and her eyes were flashing. She had never seemed as beautiful to Huck. Finally she spoke.

"I wanted to be with you, Huck," she said simply.

"My God!" he cried. "It's too dangerous in here for you. I can't let you. You've got to go back!"

"You asked for volunteers, didn't you?" Sue demanded. "So I volunteered."

Later, Old Tom was to tell Huck how Sue had volunteered. She had been on a visit to the far side of the camp when the blow came, and had returned on the run. When she learned that Huck had gone into the mine, she announced her firm decision to follow him. No talking could dissuade her, and Tom told of the futile attempt he had made to hold her back.

It was like fighting a wildcat, he said. She had slipped out of his grasp and had darted into the mine opening. It was then that a cry went up from the men grouped outside—the cry that Huck and the men inside had heard.

"Quick," shouted Huck, his teeth set, his brow furrowed. "Why did you come in here?"

"Because," she replied, and her answer was somewhat slower in coming than his question, "I would want to die if you didn't come out alive."

For a brief moment, Huck gazed down at her, then before the eyes of the men, unembarrassed, he took Sue in his arms and kissed her. Quickly, he put her aside.

"All right," he said. "Come along. No time to stop now." But he took her hand in his and they walked side by side.

Almost immediately they came upon the terrible results of the explosion. Dead men, dead mules, timbering rent and shattered, the walls of rooms blown down, side galleries blocked.

"Most of them twenty-two fellers belongs to the workin's up beyond the shaft tunnel," said Lank Mason. "There's old-timers in that crowd and they may be holdin' back for fear of choke or knowin' another blow is liable to let go if the coal happens to be afire. The force of a blow is out, not in, and choke damp gathers in the low parts fust, so they may figger they're safer up there till they know for shore what's goin' on."

Huck nodded agreement and quickened his pace. They were far into the mine, now, almost to the tunnel shaft. Suddenly he heard a sound up ahead. Somebody was groaning there, calling feebly for help. Huck broke into a run, halted abruptly. His men found him kneeling beside a man who was pinned beneath a fall of slate and timber.

The man was conscious, but his swarthy face was ghastly with pain. Huck knew all his men by sight, but his face he did not recognize. One of the foremen, dropping on his knees beside Brannon, gave vent to a startled oath as he peered into the dark, agonized face.

"What the hell's this jigger doin' here?" he demanded. "He don't work for us."

"You know him?" asked Huck, tugging at a beam which lay across the injured man's legs.

"Uh-huh," grunted the foreman, adding his strength to raise the timber. "Uh-huh, his name's Estaban Garcia and he works for Jeff Eades, Cale Coleman's drift foreman. How in hell did he get in here in this mess?"

That was what Huck Brannon wanted to know, but this was no time to question the injured man. Old Lank was pointing to the gauze of his safety lamp. It was almost redhot.

"She's gettin' bad, Huck," he said. "We better be gettin' farther in, pronto."

"Get the men t'gether and start 'em up the

lead," Huck ordered quickly. "I'll have this feller loose in another minute. Go on, I tell you, there isn't room for more'n one to work here. Go on, and keep outa my way."

Huck looked up and saw clearly in Sue's face the determination to remain, come what may, so his—

"You, too," sounded weak.

"I'll stay here, Huck," said Sue.

Huck shrugged his shoulders. "A'right, Mason," he cried, "get going."

Muttering profanity, Lank obeyed, herding the crew forward as Huck removed the last of the debris from Estaban's crushed legs. The halfbreed had sunk into a kind of stupor from pain, but his eyes showed he still knew what was going on around him.

A moment later Huck lifted the broken body in his arms and with Sue beside him started after the winking lights of his companions. He had taken less than a dozen steps when he felt a sudden ominous suck of air.

"Down on yore faces!" he roared to the men ahead. "Down, Sue!"

He saw the winking lights fall to the floor, took three long strides up a side gallery and threw himself flat, sheltering Sue with his own body and the injured halfbreed with his left arm.

There was a blazing flash of reddish light, a crackling roar and a wave of blasting heat. Huck was lifted from the floor by the force of the explosion and hurled down again. For an instant he lay stunned, then he scrambled to his knees, beating out the fire that smoldered his clothes, shaking his ringing head to clear it from fog.

"Sue," he cried anxiously, lifting her up. "Are you all right?"

"Ye-es," she replied. "Not a scratch. You?"

"Fine," he said.

He heard Lank's voice roaring anxiously and shouted back reassurance. Picking up the moaning halfbreed, he hastened from the gallery and up the tunnel, Sue following close behind.

He found that his companions had suffered more sorely than he had from the blast, whose greatest force had ripped along the main gallery.

One man lay stunned. All of them were cut and burned and bruised. Old Lank dripped blood, but he shook it from his face impatiently and went hurrying back down the gallery muttering anxiously to himself. Huck, conscious that the little stream which flowed down the gallery was spreading over the floor, motioned the others to await his return.

Soon Lank was back, his fat face grim in the flickering light of the lamps.

"Thought I heard it after the blow," he said. "Yeah, she's down—gallery blocked by a bad fall. Can't tell how far it extends, but she's liable to be plenty."

"We got tools and powder," Huck said quietly. "Besides, the boys will work to us from the other side when they find out what's happened. Come on, let's be getting higher up."

Lank glanced at him queerly, but made no comment. "Okay," he agreed heartily, "let's go."

They stumbled on up the lead, finding more and more evidence of the rending force of the last explosion. Huck anxiously watched the gauze slowly take on a pinkish hue. The fiery gas was seeping from the shattered seams, accumulating in pockets close to the roof.

Huck reckoned that they were now less than a quarter of a mile from where the lead ended at the wall built across the mouth of the dead men's cave. A plan was forming in his mind, a plan that offered faint hope for escape. For Huck Brannon knew, as old Lank had known, that, barring little short of a miracle, they were doomed.

Moreover, if ever he had been in doubt about Sue returning his feelings, the doubt was at an end. She loved him too! Now he wasn't only struggling for his own life and his men's, but for Sue's life. And that was more important to him than anything else. Now he had to get out!

He looked down at her. What a girl. Not a word out of her—not a complaint. He pressed her hand in his, and felt her respond. How cool her hand was, how steady her fingers' grip.

Even as they stumbled on, he felt a faint shock

of air follow almost immediately by a distant rumble. It was another explosion beyond the barrier of fallen roof which blocked their way to the mine mouth.

And those recurrent explosions meant only one thing: the mine was on fire and rescue from outside was impossible. Successive explosions as the gas accumulated would bring down more and more of the gallery roof, and not until the slowly rising water flooded the mine and put out the fire could the men on the outside start the work of rescue. And by that time it would not make any difference to Huck and his companions.

The Mexican miners were muttering among themselves. They too had read correctly the message of that ominous rumble. The halfbreed in Huck's arms moaned between his set teeth. Brannon shifted the burden slightly and strode grimly on.

Suddenly it was as if a mighty hand had gripped his throat, shutting off his breath. There was a taste of sulphur in his mouth, a reddish, bubbling mist before his eyes. Dimly he heard somebody coughing and gasping.

"On!" he croaked, giving a faltering man a shove. "On—higher ground."

Lungs bursting, brain swimming with agony, he stumbled forward. Sue suddenly fell beside him. Huck gripped her against his broad breast with one arm and with the other seized the halfbreed's collar. On he staggered, reeling with his double burden. He dared not risk a breath, knowing that if he filled his lungs with the deadly choke damp, he would fall and never rise. On and on, lurching drunkenly, clamping one unconscious form to his breast, hauling another over the rough floor by a spasmodic effort of the will. His swelling lungs were crushing his panging heart, stifling its beat. There was a terrific pounding at his temples, a mighty roaring in his brain. Dimly he heard old Lank's voice shouting. He opened his mouth, drew in a great breath of the lifegiving air and slumped forward on his face.

XXIV

Confession

Huck was out only a few minutes. When he recovered consciousness, two men were carrying him and Sue, whose form was still clamped in the iron grip of one corded arm.

"We couldn't pry you loose from her," Lank said as Huck was set upon his feet. "An' if that saddle colored hellion pulls through, which I don't figger he will, he shore will owe being above ground to you! You drug him 'long outa that damn choke damp after he went down."

"Never mind him," growled Huck. "How is Sue?" He kneeled down beside her.

Sue, lying on her back and breathing heavily, was showing signs of coming to. In a moment she had opened her eyes. Seeing Huck's anxious face fastened on her, she smiled up at him. It was a wan smile.

"How does it feel?" he demanded.

"Fine," she said, and started to get to her feet.

Huck helped her up.

"Hey!" exclaimed one of the foremen, "there's lights up ahaid!"

A sudden shouting arose. The party hastened forward, calling questions.

They found seven men crouched beside the wall built across the gallery. None was seriously injured.

From an old miner, bruised and burned, Huck got his first definite explanation of the cause of the tragedy.

"Eeet was an open blast," declared the oldtimer. "I hear the crackle of eet, see the flash. I know what come and throw me down on face in side gallery. The blow she mighty bad."

The others nodded, a hopeless expression in their eyes.

Stretching his arms above his head and cocking an eye at the deeping pink of his lamp gauze, old Lank expressed the general opinion.

"Well, reckon we'd might as well light up our pipes and have a comf'table smoke," he said. "Purty soon that'll set off a big blow and finish things up quick. That's better'n hangin' on till we starve or go *loco*."

The others nodded gloomy assent.

But Huck Brannon lashed out at them with a voice like steel grinding on winter ice.

"I didn't figure on hiring quitters when I got this outfit together," he said, "and I don't figure on having any with me now. Get busy with those bars and picks and rip this wall down. Move!"

They moved. Accustomed to obeying his orders without question, foremen and miners went to work. Even old Lank grunted ponderously over a crowbar and loosened two stones to anybody else's one.

Soon there was an opening in the wall. Through this opening the eighteen men filed. Sue, then Huck last with the injured halfbreed in his arms.

"Now what?" asked Lank, pausing inside the grim chamber of the dead.

Huck gestured to the end wall. "Remember how the water oozes through there?" he asked Lank.

The miner nodded.

"Which means there's one big lot of water back of that wall," Huck went on. "Which means there's a big cave of some kind there. It also

229

means that somewhere or other there's an opening to the outside. Water doesn't just grow in the ground. Even if there isn't, it's a safe bet that there's plenty of water there to flood the Lost Padre. Well, all we got to do is dig and blow the wall down and let that water into the mine. It's liable to be a hefty job—that wall must be pretty thick to hold back the weight of water against it —but we can do it."

Silence followed this announcement, but it was the silence of reborn hope.

"But s'pose the mine fills plumb up back to here?" asked one of the foremen. "Then we'll all drown."

"It won't," Huck reassured him. "The force of the water will burst a way through that fall in the tunnel and it'll drain out before it backs up this far. Anyhow, that's a chance we got to take. All right, let's get to work on that wall."

They got to work, and soon the coal was coming down in showers. They worked in shifts, the periods of labor growing shorter and shorter as the hours passed and the men succumbed to the combined onslaughts of fatigue, hunger and anxiety.

Huck Brannon, grim, haggard, tireless, was everywhere at once, urging, encouraging. He was taking a moment of badly needed rest, Sue sitting beside him, when one of the men approached him.

"Estaban, he would speak with you, *Capitan,*" said the man. "I think," he added, "that soon he die."

Huck arose and walked to where the halfbreed lay on a bed of coats. The tortured black eyes, already glazing, flickered to meet his.

"I tell before die," the halfbreed gasped. "I made gas blow. I set open blast. It go off 'fore ready—block down roof and ketch me, too."

"I figured as much," Huck told him quietly. "Why in hell did you do such a thing, Estaban?"

"I not think to kill," Estaban replied. "I think mine empty before blow. I do but to wreck mine. The Senor Coleman so order."

"Coleman, eh? So he *has* been back of all this hell raising!"

"*Si, Capitan.* He hate you, and he want mine. He know if mine wrecked by explosion and set on fire and have to be flooded, you no have money to open up again. Then he buy at own price, *si?*"

Huck nodded. "So you slipped into the mine with the other hands, placed your rotten blast and set her off? Why are you telling me this?"

The dark eyes fixed on Brannon's face. "You man! You risk life to save Estaban! Coleman know Estaban escape from pen'tentiary—do life. Jeff Eades know too. Have to do what tell. No 'fraid now no more. Damn Coleman! Damn Eades!"

With the curse on his lips, he died.

"Huck?" Lank Mason yelled at that moment, "the drill's hit water! Hadn't we better set the charges now?"

They had been driving a drill four feet ahead of the pickmen, for if the wall should be too greatly weakened and the water suddenly burst through, every one of them would be drowned before they could escape the rushing flood. Suddenly the drill shot from the hands of the man who held it. A jet of water almost as hard as steel hissed from the face of the wall. With great difficulty a plug was driven into the hole. Then the workers began driving holes into the wall and loading them with charges of blasting powder.

Finally all was ready, the last hole charged, the fuse in place. The men stepped back. Old Lank Mason's voice broke grimly on the silence.

"All right, boys," said Lank, "you done a good job, but all yore work's been for nothin'."

He pointed to the gauze of his lamp. It was almost redhot. Silently, insidiously, the deadly fire damp had seeped from the coal and filled the chamber.

"Strike a match to light the fuse and we all go to kingdom come a hell-tootin'!" said Lank. "Goin' in a minute, anyhow, if we don't put out the lamps. Looks like I won't get that last smoke after all."

"Put out the lamps," Huck Brannon said quietly.

In another moment, the last light was extinguished and the living were left with only the long rows of silent dead to keep them company in the black dark.

Sue Doyle's quiet voice broke the silence.

"I have an idea," she said. "Take your coats, soak them in the water and beat the air with them from here back to the opening you made in the stone wall. Half of you stay eight or ten paces behind the rest.

"When the front half reaches the wall, they hustle back here fast as they can and beat forward again. That way you'll drive the gas away from the wall here where we've got the blast set."

"By Gawd, Sue, that's a chance!" exclaimed Huck. "I've heard tell of that working. You can beat the damn gas back with wet bags or coats; but this roof is mighty high. I shore wish it was a low tunnel."

Stumbling in the dark the men obeyed Huck's orders, flailing away with their water-soaked coats until they reached the far wall, then staggering back to repeat the process.

Finally Huck called a halt.

"All right, that'll do if it can be done at all," he said. "Now hustle out, all of you, and up that steep gallery to the right. Lie down and cover your heads with the wet coats."

"What you gonna do?" asked Lank Mason.

"I'm gonna light the fuse," Huck told him quietly.

"And if the gas lets go, you'll be blowed to hell!" exclaimed the old miner amid a rising storm of protest. "I'm the one what'll light that fuse."

"No, me, I am the one!" shouted young Pedro angrily.

"Shut up!" Huck told them. "I'm running things yet a while. Do as you're told and don't waste time. That damn gas'll be drifting back this way pronto."

"Get goin', Sue," he ordered.

"Huck," she said, "I don't want to leave you."

"Go ahead, honey," he said. "I'll be right with you—soon as I set the fuse."

"If there's any gas left," she cried, "you'll be—" It wasn't necessary for her to finish.

"Now don't start frettin'," Huck told her softly. "Didn't we get all the gas out of here? Sure we did. Now get moving. Everyone."

Grumbling and muttering, they obeyed him, shuffling off through the dark. Huck waited until the last footstep had died away up the gallery. He gave them another minute to get snugly settled, and stooped over the fuse.

"Well, if she blows, the explosion will light the fuse and the boys'll have their chance anyway," he told himself as he scratched the match.

The little flame burned clearly, and there was no answering flash and roar. Huck touched it to the fuse-end, saw the sputter of sparks and the crawling smoulder. He straightened up, turned and raced to the gallery.

Panting for breath he flung himself down beside Sue, who gasped a muffled welcome from beneath the set coats. Her hand slopped dripping fabric over his head and shoulders and he lay with every muscle tense, awaiting the explosion.

But somehow it didn't come.

"What's wrong with it?" bellowed Lank Mason.

"Nothing," answered Huck. "It's just a slow-burning fuse." He felt Sue move beside him. "What is it, Sue?"

"Huck," she said, "before it happens—tell me—why did you leave the Bar X?"

With the sound of the sputtering fuse in his ears, Huck told Sue why he left—why he felt he had to leave.

"I had to leave because I loved you, Sue honey," he said. "And for the same reason I couldn't tell you how much I want to buy the spread over in the Apishapa River Valley."

"I know, Huck dear," said Sue. "I know . . . Listen!"

There was a crackling crash, strangely prolonged, a thudding rattle, then a mighty, roaring thunder. Huck felt himself and Sue lifted from the ground and slammed down again. There was an instant of blistering heat and a blaze of light that seared even through the wet covering that shielded his closed eyes. Then intense blackness which rocked and quivered to that rolling, unceasing thunder.

Huck sat up, flinging the wet coat aside, beating at incipient smoulders. His companions were moving beside him, but he could hear nothing because of that awful rushing thunder.

He knew what it was, however—the water released from the subterranean reservoir and rushing into the mine. Powder explosion and gas explosion had brought down the retaining wall, as he had predicted.

XXV

Iron Door

For minutes the thundering roar continued unabated; then it gradually lessened, died to a hissing rush, an intermittent gurgle. Huck fumbled a match and lit his safety lamp. There was no further danger of gas explosions with that current of fresh air which was fanning his face and pouring into the mine.

The flickering flame showed the haggard, blackened faces of Sue and his companions, but now those faces were alight with newborn hope.

"I believe you done pulled us through, feller," said old Lank, voicing everybody's opinion.

The masonry wall was completely demolished and the fallen blocks had been hurled aside, leaving a clear passage into the cave. Here the destruction was even greater.

Over to one side was a huge falling of slate from the roof, and behind and beneath the jumbled mass, sealed in an eternal tomb, were the remains of the mummified Indians and the broken body of Estaban Garcia, who had paid for his crimes with his life.

The end wall of the cavern was split from floor to ceiling—a gaping fissure through which trickled dark water and a strong current of air.

The air was pure and sweet. "And that," Huck pointed out, "means there's an opening somewhere. C'mon, Sue, fellers, let's find it."

He led the way, his arm supporting Sue, and his companions, weak from hunger, exhausted by their four-day battle in the dark, stumbled in his wake, sloshing through pools of water, climbing painfully over heaps of fallen rock.

Despite the quickened promise of life, Huck was gloomy and depressed. He knew, as Lank Mason knew, that their venture into coal mining was a failure. It would take many weeks and thousands of dollars to pump out and recommission the mine. Thousands of dollars which they did not have.

"Oh, well," he told himself at length, "I always did have a hankering for cow herding over and above anything else, but it's hard on the other boys."

The voice of Lank Mason, filled with excitement, snapped him out of his morose thoughts.

"Huck," Lank was saying, "this ain't no cave!"

"No cave?" Brannon replied absently. "Then what—"

"It's a diggin's!" Lank interrupted excitedly, "a diggin's as shore as you're a foot high. This is a old mine—a silver mine!"

His interest aroused, Huck examined the walls of the gallery along which they trudged. Lank was right. The marks of pick and drill were plain. And from time to time they passed dark openings which marked side galleries.

"Looks like she might not be worked out complete," the cowboy muttered. "This is something to think about."

They staggered on. They had been walking for nearly an hour over the muddy, water-rutted floor when Huck saw a faint gleam far ahead. Hurrying forward he saw that it came from a shaft of sunlight pouring through an opening in the gallery roof.

"We're out, Sue, fellers!" he shouted exultantly, breaking into a shambling run.

Suddenly he halted, staring, eyes narrowing with wonder.

The roof of the gallery was pierced by a slanting opening strongly paved and walled with cut stone. Its upper end was brilliant with sunshine which poured down to illuminate the gallery for some distance.

But what riveted Huck's attention was not the opening and its promise of speedy escape from the gloomy underground passages. To one side, streaked and corroded by the effects of many years immersion in water, its ponderous lock only a misshapen lump of rust, was a massive iron door with sill, jambs and lintel of cut stone.

For a long moment Huck Brannon stood staring at the unexpected portal here at the mouth of the ancient mine, his wondering companions thronging behind him. And as he stared, a possible solution of this mystery caused his blood to run wildly. Turning, he seized a sledge that had been brought along against possible emergency. In another instant the heavy hammer, wielded with all the strength of his sinewy arms, fell upon the lock. Again he struck, and again. The door creaked and groaned, flakes of damp rust showered down.

Suddenly the lock shattered, the bolt fell free from its rusted fastening. With a final crashing blow, Huck sent the door swinging open on rusty hinges that screeched shrill complaint.

Stepping forward he held his lamp high and peered into the dripping chamber which, walled and ceiled with cut stone, was of no great extent.

Old Lank, crowding close behind the cowboy, gave vent to a low whistle.

Stacked from floor to ceiling in orderly rows, were ponderous ingots, black and discolored. Huck hauled one free from its resting place of years and scratched industriously at the dull surface with the point of his knife. A clear, frosty gleam rewarded him. He held the bar for the others to see.

Old Lank whistled again, staring at the stacked ingots.

"The *five thousand bars of silver!*" he muttered. He craned his neck, swept his lamp forward. "Only there's a helluva sight more than five thousand or I miss my guess," he added. "Old Don Fernando de Castro shore weren't no piker!"

"Yes," Huck said, "this is the real Lost Padre Mine, not the one we have been working for coal."

"But how the hell," wondered Lank, "the water—the—"

"Don't you see?" Huck broke in. "That hole up there ends in the old channel they cut to let the crick run over the end wall of the canyon. The crick water filled the mine and hid it when they turned it into the channel, just as the falls hid the mouth of the other mine. Old de Castro was plumb smart. He figured if anybody did happen to spot the channel and what it meant, they'd turn the water back into the original bed and uncover the mouth of the mine down in the canyon.

"They'd think right off that they'd found *La Mina del Padre*, and when they discovered the diggings down there were worked out, they'd give up in disgust and go away. If they happened to come up this way nosing around after the water'd run out, all they'd see here would be another pool of water left when the channel emptied. Nobody'd ever suspect it as the mouth of another mine. He slipped a little in not knowing that the end wall of the gallery down below was coal and the water would, in time, seep through, and if allowed to run long enough would drain this mine. Then, of course, anyhow, he intended on coming back this way for his silver after he'd got reinforcements from Spain or Mexico.

"And," he added with a grin, "when those hellions come up here and flooded the channel again last Spring, they walked around over top of the Lost Padre silver and never knew it. And if they hadn't turned the water into the channel and filled up the mine again after it'd been draining for months, the chances are there wouldn't have been enough water in it to flood our mine and put out the fire. Gents, that's what you call justice!"

Turning, he held up the ponderous ingot in both hands.

"Take a look at this sample," he chuckled. "We all had a helluva time findin' it, and everybody's due for a cut. There'll be plenty here to pay for putting our mine back in shape, and enough left over to give every man a nice poke of *dinero*. Pedro, you can go back to *Mejico* and marry every *senorita* you're engaged to!"

"Me, I stay here in Colorado and get betrothed to some more," said Pedro, after the cheering had subsided.

"I reckon Sue honey," the gray-eyed puncher chuckled, "that that isn't such a bad idea. How about it?"

"Sounds like a grand idea to me, dear," replied Sue, her amber eyes luminous, her red lips parted.

"Then it's settled," Huck decided.

They scrambled through the opening, which, with grass and other growth fringing the edges, looked at a casual glance just like another shallow hole in the old channel bed, and headed for the canyon. It was a hard trek for starving, exhausted men, and harder for a girl, but they made it, and as the setting sun was pouring a flood of reddish light into the gorge, they burst from the growth below the site of their camp.

Men lounging about the mine mouth, which

showed evidence of the mighty flood of water which had poured from it, set up a tumultuous yelling at sight of them. Prodigious back slapping and congratulations, interspersed with a yammer of incredulous questions, followed; and the exhausted survivors were hurried into cabins for food and medical attention and rest.

As Mrs. Donovan took Sue in tow, Huck cried after her.

"Take good care of her, Mrs. Donovan, and see that she gets plenty of food and rest."

"Don't you be tellin' me what to do, me buckaroo," retorted Mrs. Donovan. "I been doin' this long before you was born."

"Where's Tom Gaylord, I'd thought he'd be here?" Huck asked of Ah Sing as the old cook plied him with steaming coffee and food, wiping his bruised and blackened face between bites and chattering away in a weird mixture of English, Spanish and Chinese.

Ah Sing's face grew long.

"Mist' Gaylold think you all dead," he replied. "He feel mighty bad— want go 'way. Man called Mist' Coleman send fo' him—say want to buy mine. Mist' Gaylold go on bullgine mebbe come hour ago fo' town. Sell mine come t'mollow."

XXVI

Hoss Flesh and Saddle Leather

Dazed as he was from fatigue, it took several minutes for that statement to penetrate Huck's brain. He stared stupidly at Ah Sing, wondering if he had really heard right. Then he realized the full significance of the Chinaman's words.

Still staring at the cook, he recalled the carefully worded agreement deposited in the Esmeralda bank—an agreement based on mutual confidence and a knowledge of the hazards of their occupation.

By the terms of that agreement, Old Tom, believing his two partners to be dead, could sell the mine and the sale would be binding. The agreement had been drawn to prevent extended and expensive litigation in just such a case as the present. Huck gravely doubted if the subsequent "resurrection" of him and Lank would void the sale, especially when Cale Coleman's wealth and influence were taken into consideration.

Face bleak, he stood up, half-reeling for a moment.

"A hot bath, and then let me sleep four hours," he told the cook. "Have Smoke saddled and bridled when you wake me up. You were right when you brought him up here from Texas, feller. I'm going to need him mighty bad!"

It seemed to Huck that his head had scarcely touched the pillow before old Ah Sing was shaking him; but after downing more food and steaming coffee, he began feeling something like his old self. His body, with the elasticity of youth, was swiftly throwing off the effects of his exhausting experience in the mine. He was still stiff and sore, but that would quickly wear off once he was in the saddle.

The big blue horse snorted gayly as Huck gave him his head. Down the canyon he thundered, onto the mesa and veered sharply into the wide Apishapa Valley. Slugging his big head above the bit, he seemed to literally pour his long body over the uneven ground. Huck Brannon, swaying lithely in the saddle, sensitive to his mount's every mood and movement, guided and encouraged, watching the stars pale in the brightening sky and counting the hours he had in which to reach Esmeralda, fifty miles away.

They drummed the dawn up out of the east, fronted the rising sun and crashed onward until Esmeralda sprawled before them on its mountain bench, uncouth and ugly in the flood of mellow light. Huck glanced anxiously at the sun, now high in the sky, and urged the straining horse to a last mighty effort.

Old Tom Gaylord's little office in Esmeralda was well filled. Two of the Lost Padre foremen were there, glowering and sullen. There were also representatives of the Coleman mines. Seated at the table across from Old Tom was Jeff Eades, vicious of mouth, uncertain of eye. Beside him was Cale Coleman, his hard face alight with satisfaction and vindictive triumph.

Gaylord was slowly scrawling his signature to the agreement of sale.

"You're drivin' a mighty hard bargain, Coleman," he complained, pausing to dip his pen in the ink as a clatter of hoofs sounded in the street outside.

"Take it or leave it," Coleman replied sarcastically.

"Oh, I'm takin' it," grunted Old Tom, bending over the sheet again. "With both my partners daid and the damn mine all busted up and flooded from floor to ceilin', there ain't nothin' I can do but take it."

"Wrong!" said a voice in the doorway.

Old Tom whirled with glad, unbelieving eyes. "Huck!" he yelled, starting to his feet. "You ain't daid then!"

Huck Brannon shook his head, his smoky eyes never leaving Cale Coleman's livid face. The mine owner's jaw was hanging slackly, his eyes had a dazed, incredulous look. Jeff Eades was white as paper, his hands were beneath the table.

Huck took a long step forward, ripped the paper from under Old Tom's pen and tore it across. He cast the fragments to the floor.

Eades and Coleman were both on their feet. "Hey, you blankety-blank-blank—" the latter howled.

Huck Brannon's cold voice cut through his yammer.

"Coleman," he said, clipping the words between his teeth. "Coleman, fifteen men died this week because of you. Suppose you try and make it sixteen! Fill your hands, you skunks!"

For a numb instant there was silence. Then the little room rocked and roared to the thunder of six-shooters.

Shot through the chest, Jeff Eades went down, coughing and retching. Cale Coleman, a wondering expression on his face, stared straight at Huck Brannon. His gun fell from his nerveless hand and the expression changed to one of horror. With a choking groan that ended in an ominous rattle in his throat he pitched forward on his face, writhed and was still.

Holstering his smoking guns, Huck Brannon swabbed the blood from his gashed cheek. Old Tom Gaylord, yammering and incoherent, but nevertheless efficient, began expertly bandaging the cowboy's streaming left wrist.

"Jest a scratch," he said, "be all right in a week."

Men were coming off the floor and from

beneath the table. Other men, shouting questions, were crowding in at the door. The corpulent town marshal shouldered his way through. He glared at Huck.

"There's been too damn many killin's here-abouts of late," he declared, "and cashin' in the town's most prom'nent citizen is too damn much. Young feller, it'll take a lot of haulin' to get you outa this mess!"

"Never mind about that, marshal," said a cold voice from the doorway. "I'll furnish all the power necessary to do the hauling. Brannon just did a job that's been needing doing for quite a spell."

"Why shore, Mr. Dunn, if *you* say so," replied the marshal apologetically, ducking his head to the rugged and frosty-eyed old figure that blocked the door. He whirled to the men in the room and jerked his thumb toward the moaning Eades.

"Haul that hellion up to the hospital," he ordered. "He ain't hurt half as bad as he thinks he is. Reckon *he'll* be able to tell us the straight of this when he starts talkin'."

But Jeff Eades was already talking, and telling *plenty!*

The office cleared and Huck told Jaggers Dunn the story of what had happened. The empire-builder listened with absorbed interest, nodding his big head from time to time.

"Of course it was Coleman who got the mountain Indians on the prod, sending his halfbreeds headed by Estaban among them. He was just a little bit too smart, though, when he had Indian drums beat every time something was going to happen. Of course the idea was to throw suspicion on the Indians, but I never knew the Indians to do so much advertising before, and it set me to thinking. But I never could get enough proof to pin anything on Coleman until now."

"You did a good job," congratulated Dunn. "Well, now everything's straightened out, I suppose you're anxious to get back to your mining?"

Huck grinned. "To tell the truth, sir, I'm about fed up on mining," he said. "With things shaped up the way they are, Lank and Tom can run the mine. Me, I been noticing that that Apishapa River Valley is mighty fine rangeland. I'm going to take my share of the money coming in and buy me a nice herd of dogies and have them run inter that valley. Going to get back into the cattle business, where I belong. Hoss flesh and saddle leather in my blood, I reckon, sir."

And Jaggers Dunn understood, and there was a wistful gleam in his frosty eyes as he watched the tall cowboy swinging lithely across the street to his big horse. For, long before he dreamed of an empire of finance and railroads, Jaggers Dunn had himself been a rider of the purple sage.

XXVII

Apishapa Spread

The dawn-cracking sun was pulling itself up by
its bootstraps in an effort to scale the chain of
mountains that ringed the Apishapa River Valley,
and chase the gray shadow that lay clustered
beneath the mesquite clumps and the cottonwood
groves, when two riders entered the slash that
ran through the north gap.

For a moment they stood their horses, then
they smiled at each other, picked up the reins
and started moving down the trail that led to the
heart of the valley.

Their sure-footed ponies, at times snorting and
squealing when they would slide stiff-legged
down a rocky pass in the trail, brought them safely
down to the floor where the river ran. The horses
picked their way leisurely along the banks of the
silver stream, sometimes fording it for better
footing. At times the trail that led through the
valley joined them and they rode it together.

The sun in the meantime had heaved itself
above the mountain tops and had touched off a
burst of gorgeous yellow color that seemed to

leap like a living flame on all sides of the riders.

Presently, they came to a large open and even rolling clearing that stretched away from them for miles. Tall grass and smooth river flowed through this immense clearing. The riders stopped beneath a shady, wide-spreading elm, from whose branches came the full-throated song of a thrush, bursting with gaiety and verve. They listened attentively for a moment. Finally one spoke.

"Our ranch will stand there, Sue," he said, flinging an arm up in the direction of the clearing. "Plumb in the center." He grinned down at his companion.

"Near the river, Huck," she said. "And it will have a flower garden, with trellis—" She smiled up at Huck.

And he found the smile so irresistible that he kissed her.

Center Point Publishing
600 Brooks Road ● PO Box 1
Thorndike ME 04986-0001 USA

(207) 568-3717

**US & Canada:
1 800 929-9108**
www.centerpointlargeprint.com